A TRUE LOVE NOVELLA

Books by Renée Allen McCoy

From The True Love Novellas Series
The Christmas Beau
Single, Saved, & Searching
A Test of Faith (Forthcoming, Book 3)

The Fiery Furnace Series
The Kiss of Judas
Confessions
The Eleventh Hour

Stand-Alone Title
In the Presence of My Enemies

Non-fiction
Soul Ties: Breaking Up with a Past That's Killing Your Future

The Christmas Beau

A TRUE LOVE NOVELLA

Renée Allen McCoy

FaytheWorks
Together in Christ

FaytheWorks Publishing, LLC
Faith works together in Christ.

Brandon, MS 39047
www.FaytheWorks.com
mail@faytheworks.com

The Christmas Beau
© 2012 by Renée Allen McCoy

This book is a work of fiction. Names, characters, places (specifically noted: Lewiston Springs, MS) and incidents are either products of the author's creativity or used fictitiously. Any resemblance to actual events or locales or persons, living or dead, is entirely coincidental with the exception of God, Jesus Christ, and the Holy Spirit: They are real. Although this body of work is fictional, the Holy Trinity is not.

Acknowledgments

Thank you, Father, for saving my soul through Your Son, Jesus Christ, by aid of Your Holy Spirit. May the world realize that Christmas is a time to celebrate the Savior's birth and understand the Sacrifice You made:

For God so loved the world that He gave His only begotten Son, that whoever believes in Him should not perish but have everlasting life (John 3:16).

Thank you to my family and friends for your continued support—I pray God's best for you all. The seeds sown, whether in heartfelt words or in kind deeds, I can honestly say was received on good ground.

Thank you readers ... those whom I do not know or may never meet face to face; I appreciate you spending some of the valuable time God has afforded to you on reading my work. I pray that some situation or conversation covered in the book helps you in your own life and/or the lives of those you know. I enjoy writing to entertain, but more importantly to direct people to God. He holds the answer to anything that you could ever ask. Try Him.

I hope you enjoy reading *The Christmas Beau* as much as I did in writing it. Love is a beautiful thing. When you have it, be mindful to cherish it.

The Bible is still the greatest story ever told.

In His Name,
Renée Allen McCoy

For all who had the courage to love again...

There is no fear in love; but perfect love casts out fear, because fear involves torment. But he who fears has not been made perfect in love.

1 John 4:18

Chapter One

Festive ornaments gracefully trimmed the Maxwell household. The fireplace mantel served for the home of evergreen swags, delicately scented pillar candles, and three oversized stockings in the classic red and white color scheme displaying those timeless words: Faith, Hope, and Love. Just inches shy of scraping the vaulted ceiling's incline stood a marvelously adorned tree with attractively gift-wrapped boxes arranged neatly beneath it. Amazingly, the elegant décor appeared to have been decorated by an interior design professional, not a busy mother.

"Grits ... fruit salad ... his favorite brand of orange juice," the woman with a green apron tied securely about her waist mumbled aloud. "I think I have everything," she stated purposefully with a finger resting upon her lips, and then peered up towards the ceiling, "except for my daughters." After flipping a switch on the fourteen-cup, stainless steel coffeemaker, she unraveled the strings from the small of her back and tossed the apron aside.

Soon, the aroma of freshly brewed Colombian coffee mingled with the appetizing smell of homemade cinnamon crumb cake muffins and a pan seared turkey bacon and sausage breakfast casserole. The dining room table was set for nine with long stem glassware awaiting servings of the sparkling non-alcoholic mimosa. Instrumental Christmas hymns softly played in the background. It was the beginning of December, the most wonderful time of the year.

"Are you going to stay in bed all morning?" Elisha's overbearing, otherwise chipper, voice invaded Charity's morning slumber. "Mama made breakfast, so you need to be downstairs in five minutes or she's going to have a conniption."

Charity jotted open one eye with her face still partially covered by the cushiony oversized body pillow she was sprawled across. After an invigorating yawn with extended arms, she managed to sit up in the bed to acknowledge her sister's command.

"Well, good morning to you too." Charity half-smiled at Elisha who was now dutifully straightening the cream colored sheets to a matching twin bed in their childhood bedroom.

"Girl, you know Mama. If you stay in that bed one minute longer, she's going to—"

Elisha's sentence was snapped in two by a loud, repetitive pound at the door. The two startled women briefly stared at one another before Charity scrambled to get out of bed.

"Are you still in bed?" A commanding voice zipped across the beautifully decorated room. "I told both of you last night that I am expecting the mayor at nine this morning." Margaret Maxwell, the mother to four grown children and one precocious teenager, stood in the doorway with both hands propped on her slender, yet shapely hips. Her chestnut colored eyes swung like a pendulum back and forth between her daughters, Elisha and Charity.

"Mama, it's only eight-thirty," Charity dared to speak out of turn.

Elisha stared at Charity who had quickly realized her outburst and braced for the impending wrath of Margaret Jean Maxwell, Attorney at Law.

"Girl, don't you tell me what time it is," Margaret demanded. She drew an erect posture from her middle daughter just by the seriousness of her voice. "Have you forgotten that your father entrusted me to entertaining the future governor of this state while he's away on business?"

Gerald Eugene Maxwell is the busy father of a spirited elementary school principal, two professional athletes, an innovative graphic designer, and a meticulous, self proclaimed up-and-coming sports analyst. He spends fifty percent of his time traveling the world over speaking and singing to large and small crowds as an enthusiastic minister and charismatic songster devoted to sharing the Gospel of Jesus Christ.

"I'm sorry, Mama." Charity, obviously frazzled, raked her kinky, auburn tinged hair back with short, purposeful strokes of her manicured fingers. "It's just that I haven't been home five hours yet and I'm already having a campaign meeting. I can do without politics for a while. I mean, he's already the mayor, why start so soon on trying to become the governor?"

Margaret's patience was quickly growing thin. "Charity, need I remind you about all of the people who need help not only in this city, but across the state as well? And it is not *so soon*. These things take preparation and the sooner the better."

"But I'm tired," Charity groaned. She crossed her arms and resignedly sighed. "Elisha can help you entertain him."

Elisha parted her lips to deliver a sharp remark to her sister's pompous rant, but before she could say anything their mother sounded off instead, "Charity Régine Maxwell." Margaret always called her children, any one of them, by their full birth name in a rigid, authoritative voice whenever she was about to administer a good ole dose of *putting you in your place* as her mother Josie would say. "I am not one of your little friends. So, don't you take that tone with me, young lady." Margaret pointed at her strong-willed, twenty-five year old daughter. "Did I complain about picking you up from the airport last night at an ungodly hour having only had two hours of sleep?" she scoffed. "Don't make me go off on you this morning. Now, I expect you downstairs," she abruptly paused, looking on at Charity's leopard print tank top and barely there, black pajama shorts before adding, "with some decent clothes on."

Charity narrowed her eyes, but respectfully kept her mouth shut this time.

"There's an appropriate outfit in the closet that I bought for you earlier this week." Then as if to soften the blow she had just delivered, as she would say to her "eccentric child", Margaret added, "It's in your favorite color."

Resolved to keeping the peace, Charity folded in her lips and slowly nodded. "Yes ma'am, I'll be down in a little bit."

As soon as the wooden door slammed shut behind their impeccably dressed mother, the sisters easily let their guards down.

"Ugh! She acts like it's my fault that the flight was delayed." Charity plopped onto her old twin bed that had recently been refinished and slammed her fists down on the ruffled sheets. "Why did I even come here for my vacation?" She grunted again as she firmly crossed her legs.

Elisha faintly sniggered. "Because she told you to."

Charity shook her head at her beautifully made-up, apparently well-rested sister. "That's not funny."

"Oh yes it is," Elisha said with a smile as she smoothed the attractively embroidered comforter across the bed she had slept in for a finished touch. "You do whatever Mama tells you to, but always complain about it behind her back as if you're still a little girl." Elisha released a telling grunt. "If you kept her out of your business things would probably be different. You don't see me broadcasting everything to her," Elisha then giggled as she added, "Well, not anymore. I learned my lesson about that. It's a good thing that I live way across town now."

Charity pondered her sister's words, knowing all too well that they were indeed true. Ever since their mother had paid off her interest-bearing student loan two years ago so that she could qualify to get a place of her own out of state, Charity felt forever indebted. Especially since the student loan was for an education she wasn't using to earn a living. She would've asked their father, even though the money would have still come out of a joint account her parents shared, it would have made for an easier request. But Gerald was in Honduras at the time and they had been advised that he should only be disturbed in the cases of emergencies. To Charity *it was an emergency*, but dared not challenge the instruction her father had given.

And then there was the time she had to solicit the services of her mother because an ex-boyfriend, unbeknownst to her, stole items from a store while they were out shopping together. Charity was facing a charge that would've gone on her permanent record, that is until Margaret stepped in and had the case dropped.

"Elisha, you're the dutiful daughter who can do no wrong. If you had dropped out of a teaching program two months before graduation, Mama would have surely found an excuse to make it okay. But for me," Charity momentarily pressed her lips firmly together while rolling her eyes before she added, "it meant that I had my head in the clouds."

Elisha smiled as she gently swiped a section of her long, silky, black hair behind her ears to clasp a borrowed pair of their mother's signature pearl earrings. "Now, you know it's not like that."

"Yes, it is," Charity snarled, looking the picture of her father with creamy brown skin and identical deep dimples. "Face it, you're her favorite—"

"She has no favorites," Elisha quickly interjected.

Charity placed a hand on her hip and looked her sister up and down. "*Oh really?* I mean just look at you. You dress alike, talk alike, *and* look alike," she added as she paced the room with her bare feet. "You don't ever hear her asking me to go shopping with her or out to lunch."

"Whatever." Elisha rolled her eyes upwards and simply sighed. "You don't even live here." She then looked away from the frameless, oval vanity mirror and modeled the earrings in her sister's direction. "Do they look all right?"

"Elisha, the earrings look fine." Charity then smirked as she said, "They look the same way on Mama."

Elisha sucked her teeth and casually waved her sister off.

Charity continued, "You know, once I get enough money saved up to pay her back, she'll see that I don't need her bailing me out any more like I'm still a kid."

Elisha released a guffaw that made her sister flinch. "And where do you plan on getting that kind of money? Girl, please. Just get dressed and meet us downstairs." She flattened her hair with subtle pats from her palms and looked back to her sister. "Really, it's not that bad."

"Let you tell it," Charity said as she pulled her stuffed suitcase towards her. "You're only going to be here until just after he arrives. I have to sit in on their entire *boring* meeting and then go to *an even more boring* press conference."

"Well, I have a function at the school. You know how I love supporting my kids." Elisha wistfully smiled and then peered into the mirror for one final touch-up on her flawless make-up. "Anyway, the mayor will probably only be here about an hour or so. And with the press conference all she needs you to do is show your face. Come on, you know that Daddy, Joshua, and Zachary are all busy and she needs us. *Especially now.* And I *will* be there after I help my staff set-up, so you won't be there alone."

"If she needs us so badly, Elisha, then why isn't Joy here this weekend?"

"Now Charity, you know that Joy had this weekend planned with her best friend since August. Besides, you know how we were our senior year in high school. Mama just wanted to let her off the hook this *one* time." Elisha held up a single finger to emphasize her point.

Charity sighed and rolled her eyes. "I wish I had a best friend to bail me out of this."

Elisha giggled. "Like I said, it's not that bad. Trust me, it's easier to just keep the peace. With Daddy gone until next week, you won't have him to hide behind."

Charity had always been considered a daddy's girl. Although she was the middle daughter to her twenty-nine and seventeen-year-old sisters, she was deemed his favorite. Maybe it was because the two had so much in common just like she had said about Elisha and their mother. Charity and Gerald were both creative minds who thought out of the box. It's a wonder how he made a perfect match and lifelong companion to the tenacious prosecutor.

"Besides, you know you want to see Milton."

"*Milton?*" Charity's voice spilled with a mixture of astonishment and apprehension.

"Yes, *Milton*. You know how Mr. Grayson loves to have his family around him during the holidays." Elisha then looked into her sister's eyes that mimicked that of a deer caught in headlights. "You had to know ... right?"

Charity shook from her daze and quietly responded, "Uh ... no. No, I didn't know." Her eyes drifted to the bay window ahead. "He wasn't here when his father was re-elected a couple years ago."

"I know. During the election celebration his father said something about him being stationed overseas." Elisha then grabbed her lightweight sweater jacket. "And you know that he's a decorated officer now."

Charity sat back down on the bed. "Yeah, I heard about his purple heart medal. It was practically all over the news."

"Yeah, CNN had great coverage on his story." Elisha smiled as she grabbed her cell phone from the vanity desk and dropped it inside her satchel handbag. "The kids at my school call him a hometown hero. They wrote letters thanking him for his military service. And everyone at our school signed this *humongous card* and sent it to him." Smiles surrounded her reflective statement.

"Well, I'm sure he liked that," Charity's words were deliberately slow. She remembered the day she heard the news almost two years ago: *Milton Lamar Grayson, wounded in the line of duty.* It was to her relief that he narrowly escaped the plane that was shot down. Not only had Milton miraculously escaped with a bullet wound to his shoulder and a minor case of internal bleeding, he was also able to drag a fellow officer to safety.

"And I'll be able to thank him personally this morning for sending those items to the school. I wasn't sure where the funds for special projects were going to come from this year, but God blessed us with Milton. That man has the heart of God in him." Elisha smiled.

"I'm glad that he helped you guys out. I never said that he wasn't generous." Charity gently crossed her arms and looked away. Her eyes glossed over in nostalgia as many familiar emotions invaded her heart.

"Are you still upset about that woman?" Elisha questioned, pulling Charity's full attention back onto her. "Why don't you just let it go? He has."

"What are you talking about?" An expression of curiosity was etched onto Charity's face.

"He's changed *and* he's single." Elisha winked as she lightly sprayed a mist of perfume on each side of her neck.

"How would you know that he's changed?" Charity scowled. "And who cares if he's single?" Her voice was stern, but not entirely convincing that she didn't want anything to do with Milton.

"I thought you guys were at least friends now. Didn't he call you back when Grandma died?" Elisha probed.

"No, he didn't call."

Elisha twisted her lips to one side. "Are you sure that wasn't around the time you had changed your number?"

"I didn't change my number until a week *after* you told me you had given it to him. It doesn't take that long to pick up the phone." Charity shifted her eyes away from her sister again as she smartly said, "He managed to call you as soon as she died didn't he?"

"Now you know that we were friends in high school and college before you two ever really got to know each other."

"I didn't mean it like that."

"I know, I'm just saying that Milton was a good friend and that's why we talked. Believe me, I gave him a hard time about the way you guys had broken up, but he did apologize for what happened. He wanted to talk to you, but didn't know your number. I had to give it to him." She then said with a smirk, "But with the way you changed your number so much back then, *I* could barely keep up."

Charity sucked her teeth. "It wasn't that bad."

"Yes, it was. And when you were home for the funeral, I'm sure he didn't want to call the house and have to deal with Mama. He may not have been her favorite or on good terms with you, but after he sincerely apologized for the way things happened between you two, he was cool with me."

Charity remembered how Margaret always ranted about Milton not being the man for her. In Charity's eyes Margaret never really gave him a chance, but after Milton did what he did Charity began to understand why her mother felt that way.

"Since then, you know we never talked again other than through emails here and there. I'm sure he would've contacted you *if* you would've let him."

Charity's heart reluctantly softened to what Elisha had just said. Although her sister knew nothing about the depths of her relationship with Milton, Charity wanted to make it clear that she was done with him. "Well, I'm only meeting with the mayor because of Mama. You know how badly she wanted to become our city's first female African American District Attorney. And being in good with the mayor, or future governor like she says, was one of the reasons that she now is."

"Oh yeah right, Charity … it's *all* about Mama now." Elisha grinned and gently shook her head. "Well, if it's like that, then you won't mind that Mama made you Milton's leading lady in the play she's got planned for the Christmas gala she's hosting at the end of the month."

"*Mama wants me to be Milton's leading lady?*" Charity tried to make sense of why Margaret would do that. "Are you talking about that script she had me look over last month?"

Elisha smiled. "That would be the one."

Charity folded her arms across her chest as she shook her head. "She emailed that to me in order to get my input on how to make it more relatable to younger people. Just like how she said she had sent it to you. You know, to punch it up a bit since an older lady from the church had written it." Charity propped her hands onto her hips. "How am I supposed to remember lines to a play now? *And* she never asked me?"

"Well, you know Mama. You were always good at memorizing lines that took me forever to get." Elisha laughed. "Besides, it's a short play that'll only take about a total of thirty minutes to perform. It'll be incorporated into the cantata. Not very traditional, but very entertaining," Elisha rambled.

"Yeah, thirty minutes to perform, but I'll probably have to rehearse for a solid week."

"Try two weeks," Elisha wiggled two fingers in front of her face.

"*What?* Why do they try to do so much at the last minute?"

"Well, not every day of course. But when we did this play last year with Janell that's about how long it took to rehearse for an hour or so after work hours."

"But I'm off."

"Well, not everybody is, Charity," Elisha said in a voice that drove her point home. "We can't all arrange our own schedule, *Ms. Graphic Designer.*"

Charity smiled at Elisha's new title for her. This was the first year Charity had actually turned a profit in her small business. The first year she could let her odd jobs go and leave her substitute teaching a distant memory. It felt good that everything she had wanted was finally falling into place. Everything except a man who was faithful to God and truthful to her.

"Humph, I wasn't planning on spending my vacation this way ... memorizing lines." Charity shook her head and sighed. "She only asked me to do the print designs."

"Hey, I was just giving you a heads up. You can say no, but my guess is that she'll probably ask you in front of Mayor Grayson. And you know print designs for you are a snap."

Charity shrugged as she nonchalantly nodded. "Does Milton know about this?"

"I don't know, but from what Mama told me on the way to the airport before we picked you up, he's supposed to be here until New Year's too. *Sounds like match-making to me.* If you want nothing to do with him it'll be better to just have Mama get our cousin, Janell, to do the part again. Mama has her on standby. She does have a copy of the updated script. She did a good job last year, but since she just got married and everything Mama doesn't want to bother her," Elisha explained. "Although, I'm sure she'd be okay with doing it again, that's *if* you want nothing to do with him."

Elisha raised an eyebrow before walking away in her simple, yet stylish ensemble.

Charity's mouth hung open as Elisha disappeared to the other side of the door. It came as an unwelcome surprise that she was expected to spend most of her time around a man whom she had dated her senior year in high school, but also parted ways on a sour note. He had graduated high school with Elisha four years prior and around the time of the break-up, he had just completed classes for an undergraduate degree. The romance had abruptly ended the night before Milton left for basic training in the Air Force. Everything was going as planned when he had completed his degree so that he could enter the Armed Services as an officer, but this particular evening something went awry.

It was a night Charity would never forget, although she had desperately tried to so many times before. They hadn't seen each other face to face since then, but coincidentally they were both visiting in their hometown at the same time.

After a few moments of thinking, it no longer seemed like such a coincidence to Charity that her mother wanted her home for Christmas this year. Margaret knew that Charity often came home to visit during Thanksgiving, but this year would be different. The mayor had a month long celebration planned with Margaret as one of the hosts to several events already put in place. The plans had strategically been organized, and Charity along with Milton would be a part of it.

As Charity peered into the closet that her mother had directed her to earlier, there she saw draped on a single, satin covered hanger her outfit for the morning: a sleek, purplish linen blend A-line dress with soft ruffles on the collar. Her mother had also taken the liberty of purchasing a pair of sheer, silk stockings and matching designer pumps to complete the outfit.

With thoughts of Milton rampantly racing through her mind, Charity snatched the dress off the hanger and rushed off to the bathroom at the end of the hall.

Chapter Two

"Good morning, Governor!" Margaret cheerfully greeted the mayor of Lewiston Springs, a picturesque southern city in Mississippi, as if he had already won the governor's race still years away. "Please, come in."

Mayor Laurence Grayson smiled as he entered the home. "Hello Margaret, it is so good to see you." He gently kissed her on the cheek as her soft shoulder length hair brushed against his face.

"Likewise." This would be the first time that he had visited the Maxwell home since the passing of Josie Henderson, Margaret's mother, two years ago. "I enjoyed that introduction." He chuckled heartily as they stood in the foyer with the door still partially open. "There's power in the tongue." He pointed at her approvingly.

"That's the truth, Laurence." Margaret nodded knowingly and then chuckled. "Will Francine and Kim still be joining us?" she asked, peering behind him to the outside.

"Oh no, she wasn't feeling well this morning. And my daughter stayed at home to look after her." He momentarily frowned, but then brightened as his son walked up and placed a hand on his shoulder. "But Milton is here."

"And I brought a hearty appetite," Milton chimed in with his distinctive laugh. "How are you doing, Mrs. Maxwell?" He slowly reached out to her and they hugged.

"I'm just fine, Milton. Thank you for asking. It is so good seeing you again." Margaret held Milton's hand as she does her own sons after a warm greeting. "When your father said that you would be home this month on leave, I just had to have you over."

Already apprehensive about coming to the Maxwell home, Milton briefly looked at his father and generated an expression that barely masked the questions he had bubbling inside. He then slowly turned back to Margaret. "Well, I'm glad that you did. It's good to see you again."

Margaret smiled at Milton as she closed the front door behind the two gentlemen, remembering the days when he used to date her daughter. He hadn't always been her choice as a boyfriend for Charity, but the two became an item anyway. Regardless of Milton's family background, the age difference between him and her daughter bothered her back then. Charity was only seventeen years old and Milton was a college senior. Although not an issue today, seven and a half years ago it just didn't seem natural to Margaret for them to date one another. She felt her daughter had a little growing up to do and furthermore with the reputation Milton had, she didn't want him sowing his oats with Charity.

Milton, although from a prominent family, used to be known as a playboy and somewhat on the conceited side. She remembered the days when Elisha would come home for a visit from college talking about the many girls he had swooning over him like he had when they were in high school. And Margaret was not going to have any daughter of hers seen as a groupie to anyone. Image meant a lot to her and the reputation of her family was not going to be put in jeopardy by anyone. She was Assistant DA at the time and well respected in the community. Now considering the path Charity had gone down by dating hoodlums and thugs who had no home-training, Margaret regretted the extent she had gone to keep them apart.

Margaret, Gerald, and Milton's parents, Laurence and Francine, had all gone to the same high school as their children. Similarly, both couples had decided to return back to Lewiston Springs after college and raise a family in their hometown. Although their past was a troubled one, it was well on the road to recovery.

"Dad has been talking about your cooking all week long, Mrs. Maxwell. I can't wait until the big Christmas party."

"Now, now, son. We'll talk business later," Laurence said, quieting Milton. Then he looked to Margaret with a telling smile and admitted, "But I have been talking about your good cooking. The spread you had at the community center when your twin sons both went pro was the talk of the town. And of course the victory dinner you prepared for my campaign team."

"Well, thank you so much, Laurence." Margaret's smile beamed from ear to ear.

"How are the boys? I hope the rivalry isn't too bad." He laughed as he referred to the opposing NFL teams her sons played for. "The season is shaping up pretty nicely for both teams."

Margaret, proud of her twins, was happy to say, "No, the rivalry isn't bad. They're both level-headed young men whose wives keep them pretty grounded." She giggled.

"That's good. Tell them I said hello."

"Me too," Milton cordially added.

"I will. Well, if you two are hungry, we can eat now if you like." Margaret just loved to cook and see others enjoy food she had prepared. Perfecting her culinary skills with each meal as well as decorating was her favorite pastime.

Laurence parted his lips to answer just as Milton said, "Uh, Dad is a little slow in responding, but you don't have to ask me twice." Milton grinned as he positioned a hand across his abdomen. "Where can I wash up?"

Laurence smirked at Milton.

Margaret replied with a smile, "Everything is still the same." She then pointed to the half-bathroom a few yards away. "There are fresh towels underneath the sink just in case Joy used up the paper towels." Margaret made mention of her seventeen year old daughter. "Teenagers are a unique brand of people and my daughter is no different. She's just like how her sister was at that age."

Milton gently folded in his full lips, knowing that she was referring to Charity. "Well, I'll only be a minute."

"See that you are because that delicious smell is teasing me." Laurence delivered a heavy pat to his son's back as he started to walk away.

"Just meet us in the dining room when you're done, Milton." Margaret then looked to Laurence and guided him through the entryway that led into the kitchen. "You know, I don't mind if you use my kitchen sink to wash your hands, Laurence. I'm not particular about that."

Laurence grinned at how down-to-earth Margaret was outside of the courtroom. She was a no-nonsense lawyer and had always managed to win her cases. She was tough, garnering respect throughout the city.

"You're not like my wife. She believes that the kitchen sink is for washing your dishes and the bathroom sink is for cleaning your hands ... unless you're cooking or something." He chuckled and then said, "In my book, dirt is dirt."

"I agree." Margaret added to his laughter as she squeezed a dime-sized amount of liquid soap into the palm of her hand and rubbed vigorously.

"What's so funny?" Elisha entered the kitchen and placed her purse onto a barstool.

Laurence looked at Elisha and smiled. "My goodness, Elisha, you get prettier and prettier every time I see you."

Elisha blushed. "Thank you, Mr. Grayson."

"How's everything going at your school? I've been hearing great things from parents in the district." He placed his arms around her shoulders and gave a tight squeeze.

"Things are great." Elisha gently patted his back as their hug separated. "As a matter of fact, we're having a Christmas jamboree slash book fair this morning."

"Oh really?"

"Yes. And most of the books were donated by the authors themselves." Elisha's expression brightened even more as she suggested, "Why don't you make a special appearance after you meet with Mama this morning? We plan to be there until four today and there'll be news coverage."

Laurence considered the offer and said, "I may just do that. The children are our future and it'll be good for the parents to see my support for events like yours. That's a good thing you've started, Elisha." He looked to Margaret, then back to Elisha. "After our meeting and the press conference, we all may make an appearance."

"Two photo ops in one morning." Margaret seemed to like the idea as she winked at Elisha outside of Laurence's view while toweling off her wet hands. "That sounds great to me."

"Okay." Elisha smiled as she walked over to the sink where her mother was and squeezed soap into the palm of her hand.

Margaret touched her on the shoulder as she said, "Oh, our mayor was next in line to use the sink." She giggled, completely opposite from the firm disciplinarian who had scolded the young women only moments ago.

Laurence grinned as Milton entered the kitchen that flowed with laughter.

"What'd I miss?" Milton adjusted the watch on his wrist.

"Just small talk," Laurence answered as he took off his suit jacket. "Margaret, I think I'll wash up in the restroom, nature calls."

She nodded understandably and took his coat as he left the room.

"It is so good to see you!" Elisha hugged Milton and graciously thanked him again for the donation to her school.

"Well, it was the least I could do," Milton modestly said. "I grew up here and went to that very same school when I was little. Anything to keep the students interested in learning."

Margaret smiled as Elisha and Milton talked. He was different in a respectful and noble way; much more mature than he was years ago. Although it was good to see that the long friendship he had with Elisha from high school through their college years had been mended, Margaret knew that didn't mean things were that way for Charity. This Christmas Margaret hoped to right her wrong and bring the two back together. She now realized that she should have never meddled because her interference was the root of a horrible breakup.

It was Charity's senior year in high school when Milton took an interest in her. She had blossomed into a beautiful, young woman right before his eyes. It wasn't long before he asked Elisha to set up a date between him and her younger sister.

Margaret nervously smiled, remembering how well Charity and Milton had gotten along during that time. As she hung Laurence's coat jacket in the hallway closet, she recalled how uncomfortable their relationship had made her.

The look of regret cleared from her face as she pulled in a deep breath and exhaled. Margaret walked back towards the kitchen and tugged at the corners of the dining room table cloth as she passed through that room. She peered upward and then nodded to herself. She had to accept what had already happened. After all, there was nothing she could do to change the past ... no matter how badly she wanted to.

"So, how do you like living back in Lewiston?" Milton cleared his throat. "I mean, I know you've been here for a few years now, but we haven't had a chance to talk in a while. How are things?"

Elisha gently smiled as she answered, "Things are good. I really like my career and since buying a house, I feel really solid right now."

Milton nodded. "I understand that. Hopefully, I'll be able to settle in one place and buy a house myself. But I don't see that happening for another few years or so."

"All done," Laurence announced as he reentered the kitchen, breaking the conversation between Elisha and Milton that Margaret wanted to hear more of.

She stubbornly tore her attention away from the two and grabbed a couple of oven mitts. "Okay, just let me pull the casserole out of the oven." Margaret then turned back to Laurence. "Please, go on into the dining room while we finish preparing things. I have your favorite breakfast drink already on the table."

Laurence's eyes widened as he nodded at her. "Margaret, you are a woman with many talents. I tell you."

"Thank you, now go on." She waved him away with a mitt. "We'll be in shortly."

He smiled and walked into the dining room. After pouring a glass of the tantalizingly smooth drink, he stood near the attractively dressed window and admired the great outdoors.

"Elisha, help me carry the food to the table."

"Oh, I can do that," Milton offered.

Margaret shook her head. "No, you all are guests in our home. We've got this covered. Now, you go on too." She playfully scooted him along.

"Just do what she says." Elisha giggled as she picked up the insulated bowl of grits and carried it into the adjoining dining room. Milton smiled at them both as he followed Elisha's steps.

Margaret took another brief moment for herself. She uneasily drew in a shallow breath before picking up the casserole and carrying it into the dining room.

"I like what you and Gerald have done with the backyard." Laurence pointed to the gazebo a few yards away. "That's a nice touch."

"Well, you know Gerald. Lately, he has been living life to the fullest." Margaret sat the warm casserole down on a padded portion of the table. "I'll be glad when he gets home. His touring has been a bit much for me this year, but thank God he's decided to take next year off."

"I can understand that." Laurence smiled. "Sometimes you just need a break."

"Yes, and with Joy preparing for graduation to go off to college, we need him here." Margaret removed the place settings she had set for Francine and Kim. "Oh, is Councilman Martin still joining us?"

Laurence looked as if he had just remembered some-thing. "Yes, he'll be here. Just a little late. I received a call from him on my way over." Councilman Gregory Martin was a prospective Lt. Governor for Mayor Grayson when he runs for Governor in the next race. "And his wife is expected to be here as well," he added.

Margaret smiled as she said, "Oh good, then all of this food won't go to waste." She pulled the foil off of the casserole dish. "My children are so particular about leftovers. *Especially breakfast food.*"

"Well, no worries, Mrs. Maxwell. I'll be glad to take it off of your hands," Milton joked.

The four of them erupted into laughter as if they'd never shared a cross word with one another. It was Margaret's mission to mend the unspoken brokenness between the two families. She had promised Gerald that this meeting would be more than just a political one, but rather an opportunity to put the past behind them and move on without any lingering misgivings.

Charity stood at the bottom of the staircase, peeking around the corner. She caught a glimpse of Milton who looked better than she had remembered. Her eyes moved from the curvature of his full lips down to the mounds of muscles that rested beneath his wool-cashmere blend gray sweater. The casual black slacks he wore stretched down to his leather loafers that complimented his outfit perfect-ly.

Charity shrunk back behind the wall and stole another glimpse of her reflection in a nearby mirror. Her hair and skin practically glowed. If she could only remedy the stubborn bags beneath her eyes everything would be perfect, but it was too late for that now. If she had only known that Milton would be here, she would have been a little better prepared.

Charity stared at herself and fought the developing tears that threatened to make an appearance. *Not today, not now,* she thought. She had to be strong. She had to show Milton that she was okay and a much stronger woman today than she was seven years ago. She had to be the confident young woman she was when he had first pursued her.

"What are you doing?"

Startled, Charity looked away from the mirror and faced Joy. "Would you stop sneaking around," Charity whispered to her youngest sibling. "Why do you do that?"

"Whatever." Joy smirked as she casually smoothed the ponytail on top of her head.

"I thought you were going to spend the weekend with Michelle." Charity straightened the thin belt around her waist.

"Well, I was." Joy rolled her eyes upward before narrowing them back onto Charity. "Her boyfriend called and they made up. So, she ditched me and our little trip for him. Something about spending the day together. You know how that goes." Joy dumped her overnight bag onto the hardwood floor. "But I'm glad you're home, Sis! What, all fuss and no hug?"

Charity released her preoccupation with Milton and smiled at her sister. "Come here, girl." She opened her arms and the two gave a tight hug to one another.

"Joy, is that you?" Margaret called out from the other room.

"She can hear me a mile away." Joy giggled and walked toward the direction of her mother's voice. "*Yes mom*, I'm home!" She pulled Charity by the hand and said as she entered the dining room, "Look who I found hiding in the hallway."

Charity's eyes met with Milton's for the first time in years. He gazed at her with his lips slightly parted. He then looked to his father with a bewildered expression splashed across his face. Questions seemed to pour from his eyes.

As the room seemed to swell with a deafening silence, Joy exclaimed, "Oh good, I'm just in time for breakfast!"

Margaret was grateful for Joy's invasion. By the look on both Charity's and Milton's faces, an interruption was needed. "Go wash your hands and we'll have prayer."

As Joy left the room, Milton staggered in Charity's direction. "It's so good to see you." He reached for her, but she simply raised her hand. Ignoring her cold shoulder, Milton hugged Charity anyway.

"It's good seeing you too." Charity mastered the art of disguise, quieting any unwelcome comments from her mother. However sour things ended between them it felt confusingly good having Milton close to her again. "So, how long have you been home?" Charity gently pushed him away.

"Well ..." Milton slowly smiled in the direction of his father before turning back to answer, "Since yesterday. I'll be here until the first of the year."

Charity's eyes narrowed. "Oh ...." She then peered at her mother before looking back at Milton. "Me too."

The two nervously chuckled.

"I'm done." Joy reentered the room. "Are you going to pray, Mama?"

Margaret slid her eyes away from her youngest child and asked everyone to join hands. As they gathered around the rectangular dining room table, Charity tried to avoid physical contact with Milton again as she reached for her sisters' hands. But somehow he ended up next to her, slipping his hand over hers.

Respectful enough not to cause a disruption before approaching the throne of God, with a sigh Charity allowed her fingers to intertwine with Milton's. It was almost like old times. He still had a piece of her broken heart. Although she has had two boyfriends since they had parted ways, neither one of them could hold a candle to Milton Grayson.

Milton stood in the prayer circle, peering down at Charity's slender fingers. She had always been a petite woman with a graceful air about her. Although he had been good friends with Elisha who some had confused for his girlfriend, it was Charity that held his heart.

As Margaret said, "Amen," Charity quickly moved away from Milton and took a seat on the opposite side of the table. Looking on at her fleeting glances, Milton understood Charity's standoffish behavior.

Everyone sat down at the table and ate before any formal business was discussed. Once conversation about the Christmas gala began, Joy was excused. Elisha offered her input as to the program participants she had secured, a Christian comedian and a young Gospel group who would perform two song selections, before she had to leave for her event at the school.

Laurence confirmed that his wife would deliver a brief discourse about the meaning of Christmas where his daughter would be a backup for her. Charity agreed to design the program guide and miniature party favors with seasonal greetings glorifying the Savior. And barring any travel delays, Margaret informed that Gerald would offer a solo from his soul-stirring Christmas album, *Our Glorious King Has Come.*

"This is going to be a great Christmas, I can just feel it in my bones," Margaret said, hopeful about the time she'll have to spend with her family this month. "Although I won't have my boys with me on Christmas Day, I thank God their schedules may allow them to fly in for a day or so this month. Anything the Lord gives me, I'm grateful!" To look at her, Margaret appeared very prim and proper, but when it came to the Lord and Savior Jesus Christ, she could hardly contain herself. Much like her husband, although not so much in the past, the two now aimed to please God with everything in them. From the love and respect they showed one another to the way they raised their children. It was certainly a God-centered household.

"I'm right there with you, Margaret. I want the people of this city to know that it's not just about politics, but it's about giving back. The turkey drive for Thanksgiving was just the beginning. Once I announce the food and toy drive to give away at the community luncheon, I'm sure the meaning of Christmas will come through loud and clear."

They both smiled and pointed at one another, reciting the focal Scripture from Sunday's sermon delivered by their pastor, "Matthew 25:35-36," which states: *for I was hungry and you gave Me food; I was thirsty and you gave Me drink; I was a stranger and you took Me in; I was naked and you clothed Me; I was sick and you visited Me; I was in prison and you came to Me.*

"Are we late for service?" Councilman Martin asked, chuckling with his wife on his arm. "I thought this was supposed to be a business meeting, but it sounds more like a church service," he joked.

"Mama, I let them in." Joy stood at the entrance of the dining room behind the Martins, holding the keys to her car. "I'm going to the mall to meet some friends."

"Okay, sweetie."

Joy squinted as she quietly repeated her mother, "*Sweetie?*"

"Meet us at Elisha's school in a couple of hours." Margaret smirked as she quipped, "If you're not too busy."

"*Okay, Mom.*" Joy, reigning homecoming queen at her high school, returned a beautiful smile and waved at the others as she left the home.

"Well, come on in and join the service." Margaret stood and welcomed the councilman and his wife to the seats Joy and Elisha had vacated. "And without God there's no need to have a meeting."

They all nodded and laughter once again filled the home.

As the Martins ate their breakfast, Charity gathered ideas from Laurence as to how he wanted the print designs for the Christmas party to look. She showed him samples from her growing portfolio that seemed to impress even her mother.

"Charity," Margaret started in a surprised voice, "these are really good."

Charity avoided looking at her mother, unsure as to how to take that comment. Was it that Margaret didn't have enough faith that her daughter could succeed as a freelance graphic designer or was it that she just didn't want to? With a quiet sigh Charity simply answered, "Thank you."

Milton slid the portfolio in front of him, and with raised eyebrows said, "Wow. I didn't know that you were a designer. These samples are great."

Somehow compliments about her work sounded differently coming from him. "You really think so?"

Milton took advantage of the warmth Charity was beginning to show. "Oh yeah, there's a guy I know who's retiring from the Air Force next year that's looking for someone to design a brand logo for the new restaurant he's opening." He then casually tapped her on the shoulder. "Hey, if you like, I'll give him your information."

Charity smiled and reached into her pocket book that she had grabbed from the China closet and pulled out a business card.

Milton took the card in his hands and said, "Write down your cell and I'll pass the info on to him."

Charity quickly scribbled her number down on one side of the personally designed double-sided card and handed it back to him.

"Great, I'll be sure that he gets this." Milton flipped the card from one side to the other before slipping it into his front pocket.

"Okay ... thanks." Charity reluctantly nodded, realizing that Milton had cleverly fished her personal contact number out of her. Normally, she would only provide her website and email address as printed on the card, but she was somewhat thrilled about the new potential client.

"Please, excuse me," Milton said as he peered down at his buzzing phone.

"Oh, no problem. If you need a little privacy, feel free to step into the living room," Margaret offered.

Milton's nose crinkled at the phone number flashing on his screen display as he nodded. "Uh, yes ma'am, thank you. I think I will."

Charity looked to Milton in concern. "Is everything okay?"

Milton gently smiled in her direction as he stood. "Yeah, everything's okay. I guess the word is out that I'm in town." He grinned as he pushed his chair underneath the table. "Excuse me everyone, I'll be right back."

Charity looked on, curious as to who could be calling Milton. He hadn't been her boyfriend in years, but the urge to ask who was calling him burned on her tongue. Moments passed and Milton was still in the living room, talking to someone Charity assumed to be a female. The way Milton's voice sounded before he went out of earshot confirmed that for her.

Five minutes had passed and Milton was *still* on the phone. While the business meeting continued, Charity found herself helplessly consumed by her curiosity. She discreetly leaned to one side so that she could catch a clear view of Milton across the hall. He chuckled while nodding his head. Then Charity watched as he suddenly took the phone from his ear. Barely keeping her balance in the chair, she quickly looked away as he started back in the direction of the dining room.

"I apologize for that." Milton slid his sleek phone back into his pocket. "What'd I miss?"

Charity was hoping for a clue instead of boldly asking, "An old friend?"

Milton half-smiled as his eyes shifted from her delicately glossed lips back to where he had just secured his phone. "Something like that."

Charity took that as a polite way of saying *it's none of your business*. Milton offered nothing else and she asked nothing else in the midst of her mother's peers. She simply stared down at the notepad in front of her and pondered the possibility of spending her vacation with a man who had hurt her terribly and then had the audacity to move on to another woman.

"Charity, as a part of the entertainment for the event there's a play that I'd like you and Milton to be a part of,"

Margaret proposed in front of the mayor just as Elisha had predicted. "What do you think, Milton?"

Charity reserved her response, anticipating Milton's reply.

"Well," Milton began, clearly caught off guard by the suggestion, "anything for charity."

Charity looked surprised, assuming that he was talking about her, until she realized that Milton was speaking of the charitable organization in which they were going to donate the proceeds.

Margaret looked back to her daughter with a soft smile on her face. "So, what do you say? If you can't, I understand. I know this is your vacation and all and such short notice."

Margaret knew how to play that motherly Mrs. June Cleaver role better than the co-star from *Leave It to Beaver* when in front of others. Charity cleared her throat and slowly nodded.

"Is that a yes?" Margaret's tone changed as she sought clarity as if she were trying a case.

"Yes, Mama. It shouldn't take me long to learn the lines if it's a short play."

"Wonderful. We had gotten such positive feedback from it last year when we presented it at church that I thought we'd do it again this year on a larger scale. I've already invited some people from neighboring churches to join in on the celebration."

Laurence nodded at Margaret and then smiled at the Martins.

"The ideas that you have are sure to make this one of the better Christmases this town has seen in years," Gregory said before he took a sip from his mug of hot coffee.

Margaret modestly chuckled. "Well, thank you."

With an hour already elapsed, the group finished fleshing out the final details that hadn't been covered during the teleconference in the previous month. The Martins confirmed the positive response of the Angel Tree mission project that they chaired.

The Angel Tree was where names of children whose parents were ill, imprisoned, underemployed or unemployed were placed on a large Christmas tree. Annually, patrons selected names from the tree and purchased items that were requested on the paper hearts that the receiving children had written out themselves.

"Well, I think that covers about everything. Are we missing anything?" Margaret looked at Laurence and Gregory who both shook their heads. "Okay, I guess we'll make it to the press conference a little earlier than expected. Afterwards, we can all go to Elisha's book fair jamboree." She smiled and asked Charity to help her clear the table before turning to her guests. "We'll have to meet you all there in about thirty minutes."

"No problem, Margaret. I need to check on my wife anyway. I hate that she won't make my press conference." Laurence stood and pushed his chair underneath the table. The Martins followed suit.

"Oh I know. Be sure to send my love to her," Margaret said as her eyes nervously glanced from Laurence to Charity who had just picked up the last gift, the personally engraved casserole dish, her mother Josie had given before her passing.

Laurence nodded. "I'll do that."

Looking away from Charity, Margaret said, "Well, let me get your coat and I'll walk you all out."

The Martins gave their thanks as they all walked out the room together; all of them except Milton and Charity. They momentarily gazed at one another as the empty casserole dish began to slip from Charity's hands.

"*Oh my goodness.*" Charity tightened her grip on the container that her mother often guarded. "If I break this, I'll never hear the end of it."

"I can carry that for you." Milton reached for the glass dish and paused as his hands rested over Charity's.

She gently pulled away. "Uh, that's okay. I've got it. You go on. I guess I'll see you at the press conference."

As Charity turned to walk away, Milton pulled her back by the elbow. "Please, can we talk?"

Charity wasn't ready for this conversation, but knew the moment she heard he was in town that it was bound to happen. She turned around and met his gaze again, still angered by the hurtful words he had said to her years ago. "What do you want to talk about, Milton?" Her voice had stiffened, no longer able to mask the lingering emotion.

Milton exhaled, but his words stalled. He had replayed this moment in his mind over and over, unsure if it would ever really happen. The embarrassment that gripped Charity's face on that last night they had seen each other still haunted him. He wanted to apologize for what he had done, but just didn't know how.

"Milton, I'm waiting." Charity placed the dish back onto the table and crossed her arms. "After all of these years, what do you want to say to me now?"

Milton reached for her hands and looked her deeply in the eyes. "I—"

"Oh Milton, you're still here." Margaret walked back into the room. She looked at Charity who abruptly dropped Milton's hands and then walked into the kitchen.

"Uh, yes ma'am. I was just leaving." Milton looked to swinging kitchen door before starting for the front door. "Excuse me, Mrs. Maxwell. I'll see you at the press meeting." Milton gently touched Margaret on the shoulder as he quickly walked past her.

Margaret stood motionless as she remembered the past that Charity knew nothing about. She slowly folded her arms, not wanting to come between them again.

Chapter Three

"Over here!" Elisha stood behind a rectangular wooden table decorated with colorful signs as she waved to her mother.

Despite the cloudy morning, the day had turned out to be a beautiful, and surprisingly an unseasonably warm afternoon. Coats that the children had worn to the school cluttered an area near the jungle gym on a large dark red blanket. Margaret approached Elisha with a bright smile plastered on her face. She had exchanged her heels for a lower pair of pumps and her skirt suit for a pair of slacks and a lovely blouse.

"Where's Charity?" Elisha asked as she reached for her mother's purse. "I thought you two were going to ride together," she said, stuffing the expensive pocketbook into a dollar store plastic back next to hers.

"She's on her way. We went back home to change clothes, but she said she had something to take care of and that she'd meet us here. So, I left the keys to the other car." Margaret tilted her chin down and gazed upward into Elisha's eyes. "I think she just wanted to go back to sleep, so we may not see her here today."

"Well, I hope she does make it. There are a couple of her old friends here asking about her." Elisha momentarily looked away from her mother to greet another parent who had just arrived. After the woman walked away with her child and a brochure in her hand, Elisha turned back to Margaret. "Hopefully she's not too tired to come out. It's good to have her home for a few weeks instead of just a weekend."

"Well, God does deliver miracles." Margaret instinctively smoothed her daughter's hair back into place that had been slightly disturbed by a passing breeze. "If she hasn't crawled back into bed, she just may show up."

"As we know, with God, all things are possible." Elisha grinned, remembering how Charity didn't want to get out of bed this morning. "So, how did the press conference go? I'm sorry that I couldn't make it, but as you can see we have a very big crowd."

"Oh I can see that." Margaret nodded as her eyes surveyed the schoolyard. "I'm so proud of you, Elisha. You've really gotten the children interested in reading more."

"Thank you. It took a little bit of work this year, but I couldn't do it without the great teachers we have in the classrooms."

"Yes, they are the ones on the front line. And I'm sure they appreciate how much you value them." Margaret smiled as she watched two young boys tossing a football back and forth to each other. "Hmm, those boys over there remind me so much of Joshua and Zachary when they were their age."

Elisha's eyes followed her mother's. "Oh yeah, always with a ball in their hands."

"Yes, I'm looking forward to Sunday's game. Too bad Gerald will miss it." Margaret disappointedly smiled to herself. "But I'll be happy to tell him that the press conference went well. Mayor Grayson personally invited the city to the month long of festivities planned *and* …"

Elisha widened her eyes as she leaned in closer. "*And what?*"

"*And* he announced that he's giving a sizeable donation to the scholarship program I started at the church!"

"*Wow, Mama*, that's great!" Elisha hugged Margaret in excitement. "Grandma would have been proud."

This was a program Margaret had started in honor of her deceased mother. Josie Henderson was a philanthropist in her own right, giving at times when she barely had enough for herself. She had earned a place in history as far as their community was concerned. She was a woman who had participated in sit-ins and gone to jail for simply defending her rights as a human being. Margaret would never forget all that her mother had sacrificed by working numerous jobs so that she and her siblings could have a decent education. After having buried their father at a young age, Josie remained unmarried, working even harder in the community for the betterment of others.

"Yes, she would have been very proud, Elisha. Mama drove home the fact that we needed a decent education to get a foot up in this society, and I just want to carry on her legacy." Margaret peered at her daughter as the corners of her mouth gently rose. "That's all I've ever wanted for you guys."

Elisha hugged her mother again. "I know, Mama. And—"

"Ms. Maxwell, may I use the phone to call my dad?" Elisha's sentence was snapped in two by a young boy who tugged on her blouse as he stared up at her. "He promised that he'd be here to help me pick out books."

Elisha released the embrace she had with her mother and looked to the despondent child. "Michael, where's your mother?" she asked, momentarily looking away from the child towards the tent where books were being sold and then to the tables where food was being served.

"Oh, she's over there." Michael pointed to a bench where his mother sat deeply engaged in a conversation with a man who obviously held her attention more than her child.

"Now, she knows that we don't have chaperones for today. All of our teachers are volunteers for the food, games, and book sales." Elisha quietly sighed to herself as she took the child by the hand. "Mama, could you please watch the sign-in table until I get back?" She then curtly added, "I think I need to have a little conference with a parent."

Margaret nodded knowingly. "Oh sure, I'll look after things."

"Thanks, I won't be long." Elisha marched in the direction of where Michael's mother was casually seated.

Margaret watched as Elisha seemed to be engaged in a spirited conversation with the mother of six-year old Michael. As Margaret stared at the exchange between Elisha and Michael's mother, a familiar face came into view. The woman must've been a friend of Michael's mother. Margaret was unable to place her right away, but she knew her from somewhere.

"Mrs. Maxwell?"

A familiar voice pulled Margaret's attention away from the woman. When she turned around and faced the person, a smile instantly grew on her face. "*Oh my goodness!* What are you doing here?" She covered her mouth with the palms of her hands before excitedly wrapping her arms around Gerald's broad shoulders. She squeezed them as if they hadn't seen each other in years. "I wasn't expecting you for another week!"

Gerald's wide smile couldn't be contained. "Well, for once I was able to keep a secret from you." He chuckled as Joy walked from behind him. "And I owe it to my little girl, she helped make it possible."

Margaret looked to Joy in amazement. "You knew?"

Joy gently smiled at her mother as she nodded. "Something like that. Daddy called me on my way to the mall. He was going to take a cab ..." she shifted her eyes from Margaret up to Gerald who towered over her, "but decided at the last minute to see if I was available."

Gerald placed an arm around Joy's shoulders and kissed her on the forehead. "And she gave up a day with friends to pick up her old dad."

"Oh Daddy, you're not *that* old." Joy giggled as she playfully poked her father in the chest.

"Gee, thanks Joy." Gerald chuckled as he rubbed the side of Joy's arm before taking Margaret again in his.

Joy giggled as she rummaged through her shoulder bag and pulled out her phone. "Oh Mama, when I stopped for gas on the way to the airport, I saw Mrs. Francine," she casually mentioned as she rolled her thumb across the screen of the phone.

Margaret's fingers slowly stopped moving on Gerald's chest as she gave Joy her undivided attention. "You saw her at the gas station? When was this?"

"Oh, not too long after I left home." Joy shrugged. "I tried to call out to Kim, but they didn't hear me. Why weren't they at the meeting this morning?"

Margaret passively cleared her throat as she met Gerald's gaze.

"She wasn't at the meeting this morning?" Gerald asked Margaret in a pensive tone.

"No, Laurence said that she wasn't feeling well," Margaret began, "but maybe she was out to get medicine or something."

"Maybe, but she looked fine to me," Joy said in between texting on her new phone.

"Uh Joy, could you please call Charity and see if she's going to make it here today. Elisha said that a couple of her friends asked about her."

"Okay, just let me use the restroom first," Joy answered with her eyes still glued to her phone. "I'll be right back," she said, smiling down at the lighted screen.

Margaret shook her head as Joy walked towards the building. "We're going to have to get that girl off that phone one way or another."

"I know. She's become *way* too attached to it." Gerald then hugged his wife again, this time giving her a long-awaited kiss to go along with his greeting.

Margaret's eyelashes fluttered. Gerald was still the only man she'd ever love in that way. The two had been married for nearly thirty-five years and it seemed as if each year ignited a renewed passion for one another. Subtle changes like a new gray hair here and there often went unnoticed between them as they looked beyond the surface, reveling in the beautiful spiritual bond they shared.

"*Ooo Mama*, you better not let Daddy catch you," Elisha joked as she snuck up behind her parents.

Gerald turned around and smirked at his comedic daughter.

"Oh Daddy, it's you." Elisha playfully gasped.

"Come here, you." Gerald pulled Elisha towards him and held her in his arms. "Now, you know I'm the only man for your mother." He groaned as they swayed back and forth, having not seen each other in over a month.

"Yes, I know," Elisha proudly said before she stood on the tips of her toes and endearingly pecked her father on the cheek. "Thirty-four years and counting."

"That's right and February will make it that milestone thirty-five," Gerald said before Margaret slid her arm behind the backside of his waist. "But to me, each year I get to spend with her is a milestone."

Margaret melted at his words.

"Well, I'm glad you came home early, Daddy. I'm sure the pastor will be happy to see you tomorrow. Are you going to sing a solo in the morning?"

Gerald modestly shook his head. "Elisha, the church is filled with talented songbirds. I think I may rest my pipes for a little while." He gently placed a hand across the front of his neck.

Margaret looked to him with concern as she placed her hand atop his. "Is everything all right?"

"Elisha, do you see this? All I said was that I'm going to give my voice a rest and she's already trying to treat me as if something's wrong." He chuckled heartily and peered deeply into his wife's waiting eyes. "I'm fine. It's just that I've been traveling and singing so much that I just need a little TLC. Tender, loving, care." He flirtatiously winked at his wife.

Elisha crinkled her nose as Margaret blushed.

"*Ew*, please spare us the details," Joy teased as she walked back towards her family. "I thought old people didn't talk like that."

"So we're old now? Five minutes ago I wasn't *that* old," Gerald lightheartedly reminded her.

Joy simply giggled as she gaped back down at her phone again.

"Girl, you and that phone." Elisha shook her head at Joy who just ignored her. "Do you hear me talking to you?"

Joy peered up from her phone and said, "I was sending Charity a text back."

"Oh, is she on her way?" Elisha asked.

Joy shook her head. "No, she's in bed."

"In bed?" Gerald asked in a surprised voice.

"Yep."

"Does she know that I'm home?"

"Nope." Joy looked up at him. "Did you want me to tell her?"

Gerald briefly pondered the offer, but then decided against bothering her. "If she's tired, let her rest. We'll have plenty of time to talk later."

"Okay, well I'll see y'all later." Joy giggled as she hugged her father again. "My friends are waiting for me at the mall."

"All right, but no texting and driving," Gerald firmly said. "You hear me?"

"Yes, Daddy. I hear you," Joy droned as she walked away.

"That girl is something else," Margaret said.

"Just like her mother," Gerald teased.

Margaret was much more relaxed since her husband arrived. Preparation for the press conference and the event planned at the end of the month had taken a lot out of her. She had been a little more on edge with her daughters than usual, but merely wanted things to go more smoothly with the Grayson family than they had years ago.

As Margaret's eyes shifted from Gerald's to the black Cadillac parked across the street, she saw Laurence emerge from the vehicle, now without any of his family members.

"Gerald, Laurence is here," she whispered, discreetly pulling him aside as Elisha spoke with one of her teachers. "But he looks like he's alone." They then glanced at one another.

"Was he alone this morning?" Gerald inquired.

Margaret shook her head. "No, Milton was with him. And you heard what Joy said about Francine and Kim. I wonder what's going on with them. Has he mentioned any problems that they may be having?"

"No, he hadn't said anything, but we haven't spoken in a month. And since hashing everything out years ago that happened between our families, I thought it was water under the bridge."

"I thought so too," Margaret fretted. It now seemed somewhat strange to her that while she stood supportively alongside the mayor and his son that his wife and daughter were out driving around town.

"I thought they understood our reasons for not wanting Milton and Charity together back then. It was for their own good. Not to mention what he did," Gerald said and then firmly folded in his lips.

"Yes, but maybe Francine sees things differently." Margaret helplessly shrugged, regretful that Gerald too was unaware of the lengths she had gone to keep the two apart.

Even in hindsight, Margaret viewed her actions as protective and caring, but with what happened in the aftermath, she knew others would see it as underhanded. Gerald agreed with his wife that Charity was too young for Milton at the time and thought the two had simply decided to part ways after the scandal of him being caught with another woman. But the depth of their split wasn't as simple as he had supposed.

"Gerald, when did you sneak into town?" Laurence grinned and reached for Gerald's hand.

"Not even an hour ago." Gerald chuckled as he firmly shook Laurence's hand. "How's everything going?"

"Just fine." Laurence then glanced at Margaret. "I have to thank your wife again for that wonderful breakfast. I'm really looking forward to the gala at the end of the month."

Gerald smiled endlessly as he draped his arm across Margaret's shoulders and kissed her on the cheek. "Yes, God has truly blessed me."

"Yes, He has," Laurence admitted with a hint of admiration in his eyes. "But I thought you were going to be out of the country until next week," he further questioned as a wave of confusion floated across his face.

"Well I was, but God placed on my heart that I needed to be at home." Gerald kissed his wife again as he gently rubbed her shoulders. "Marriage is a ministry too."

Laurence seemed to take the words to heart as he slowly nodded.

"By the way, how is Francine? Margaret told me that she and Kim didn't make it to the meeting. Not even to the press conference. Is everything all right?"

Margaret listened intently, prepared to read between the lines just as she does when trying a case in the courtroom. She was trained to hear the facts and decipher coded talk, although Gerald had often told her that she read too much into things outside of work.

"Well, she wasn't feeling well this morning. And then when I spoke to her on the phone she told me that she had felt a little better and tried to come to the press conference, but ended up back at home again."

Gerald nodded understandably. "Well, tell her that I'll be praying for her. I know what it's like to be sick in weather that changes from hot to cold or vice versa at the drop of a hat."

"Yes, the weather has really been up and down this season," Laurence agreed. "And thank you. I'll be sure to let Francine know that you asked about her." He then removed his jacket that was a part of the dapper suit he had worn earlier that morning and draped it across his arm.

"Oh Mr. Grayson, let me take that for you." Elisha reached for his suit coat as her fellow teacher walked away to man a food stand.

"Don't worry about it, Elisha. I won't be here long. I just wanted to show my face and let you know that I support the great things you're doing for our children." He chuckled as he surveyed the playground area. "I told Francine that I wouldn't be here long."

"Where's Milton?" Elisha questioned.

"Oh, something came up. He said to tell you that he's sorry, but he did send a little donation." Laurence pulled a check from his shirt pocket. "And here's something from our family." He then pulled some money from his wallet."

"Oh, you all didn't have to do that. You do enough in running the city," she complimented.

"We can never do too much and could always afford to do a little more," Laurence confessed.

"Well, our school thanks you." Elisha smiled endlessly as she stuffed the check and cash he had just given to her in a money bag. "And I'm sure the reporter would like to do a short interview. She spoke with me earlier when we were getting set up." Elisha glanced in the direction of the news truck that now had that same inattentive parent whom she had spoken with earlier and her son, Michael, interviewing them. "I hope she can manage to pull two sentences together that make sense," Elisha callously mumbled. "She scolded Michael for asking to use my phone instead of apologizing for not watching her son."

Margaret stared at the woman and her son, but her expression changed when she saw the other woman she had seen earlier under a shaded tree who stood not too far away from them. And then it hit her, she knew exactly who the young woman was. Margaret couldn't believe that she had changed so much. The woman's hair was longer, the body a little heavier, and her style of dress had changed, but there was no mistaking now that this was the same woman who essentially took part in breaking her daughter's heart.

"*Anita,*" Margaret uneasily whispered.

"What'd you say, Mama?" Elisha shifted her attention off of Michael's mother to her own.

Margaret shook from her gaze. "Oh, it's nothing. I was just thinking aloud."

Elisha turned away from her to greet another parent as Gerald's cell started to ring.

"Excuse me, sweetheart, it's my agent," Gerald said to Margaret. "I have to take this. Think about where you'd like to go to dinner later." He winked as he placed the phone to his ear and walked a few paces away from the group.

"Busy man, huh?" Laurence curiously said to Margaret who still appeared slightly distracted.

"Oh yes, Gerald is always busy doing something." She endearingly smiled. "Even when he's at home supposedly resting, he'll start pet projects." She casually chuckled. "But that's just who he is."

Laurence grinned and nodded. "Well, whenever he's away if you need anything done just let me know. I'm pretty handy myself."

"Well, I'll keep that in mind, Mayor." Margaret looked back to Anita who was now handing a plate to Michael's mother.

"Well, it looks as if the reporter is headed this way." Laurence adjusted his tie and quickly slipped his jacket on.

"I better get Gerald." Margaret looked to her husband who had his back turned.

"He looks pretty tied up. It must be an important call," Laurence insinuated. "We can do the interview. Besides, you spoke well on his behalf at the press conference."

Margaret sighed, tempted to tear her husband away from his agent, however, she knew that he was in the middle of negotiating a contract for a new album.

"Mayor Grayson, may we get an interview with you and DA Maxwell?" the reporter asked with a cameraman close behind her.

"Well, you'll have to ask her." He released an offbeat chuckle.

Margaret peered back to her husband again who had further lengthened the distance between them before turning back to the reporter. "How long will you be here?"

"Oh, we're wrapping things up now. We have another story to cover across town. Do you mind answering a few questions on camera? I'm sure the viewers would love to see the more relaxed side to you."

Margaret looked to Gerald again. She thought about how hard Elisha had worked to organize this event and she couldn't bear to not have her husband comment on it. "Sure, I'll answer a few questions on camera. Just let me get my husband."

The quirky reporter smiled and nodded as she motioned to the cameraman to set up. Laurence's smile faded as the cameraman steadied a tripod onto the ground. He then stared at Margaret whose hand was delicately positioned on Gerald's arm before turning back to the reporter.

"Can we do my piece now? I have to leave in a few minutes." Laurence said with a sense of urgency as he buttoned his coat up. "My wife is expecting me."

The reporter nodded as she signaled her cameraman and extended the microphone in Laurence's direction. He quickly answered her questions as Margaret and Gerald stood on the sideline. When he was finished, Laurence shook Gerald's hand and told them both that he had to leave.

Laurence briskly walked back towards his car. As he sat behind the wheel and peered through the windshield at Margaret and Gerald, Laurence pinned his lips together. He shook his head as he started the engine and backed out of the parking space.

Margaret watched as Laurence left and fell speechless. His behavior was odd, but she again was trying not to read too much into things. Before she could complete her thought, Anita came back into view. She slipped into a maroon-colored vehicle and drove out of the parking lot Laurence had only moments prior.

"Honey, are you okay?" Gerald carefully asked. "You look a little out of it."

Margaret peered into her husband's eyes and responded, "I'm just tired." She had never lied to her husband and this time was no different. Margaret was tired. Tired of carrying this thing around with her like she had for the past seven and a half years. She was just tired of it all.

Chapter Four

"What are you doing here?" Charity stood at the front door of her parent's home with folded arms. The light breeze gently disturbed the colorful peacock feather earrings that dangled from her lobes. "I thought you were going to Elisha's book fair."

Milton nervously looked off in the distance as he shook his head. "No, I mean, yeah I was going to go, but I wanted to talk to you."

"About what?" Charity's eyes narrowed as she frowned. "And how did you know that I'd be here?" Her voice took on a bitterly sour tone. There was freedom in speaking her mind since no one else was around to hear or judge her.

"I saw your mother leaving alone," Milton said in a low voice.

Charity grimaced as her eyes scaled the secluded property, finally locating his car off in the distance near the entrance of the short paved road that led to the residence. "So you're staking out our house?"

Milton sighed, and then pressed his lips together. "Now you know me better than that."

"I don't think I know you at all, Milton," Charity challenged him, raising an eyebrow now with her hands planted on her hips.

Milton nodded, understanding her stiff attitude. All throughout his military career, he hadn't once phoned to apologize or ask for Charity's forgiveness, although he knew she deserved some sort of explanation for what he had done. Many times he picked up the phone to call her, but in his mind there were no words to justify his actions from that night their relationship had ended. He had acted out of character and turned his back on the woman whom he had claimed to love.

"Aren't you going to say something?" Charity questioned, bringing Milton back into her world.

"I'm sorry," he sincerely said. "I know that I should have said that a long time ago, but I really didn't know how to face you."

"But you managed to stay in touch with my sister."

"Daddy told me about your grandmother's passing and that's when I got in contact with Elisha." Milton shifted his weight from side to side as he stood on the steps that were bordered by two large weathered statue lions on either side. "I asked about you."

"Whatever." Charity scowled, angrily rolling her eyes. "That's not the same thing."

"You're right, it's not." Milton scratched the side of his ear and then looked down to the cemented floor of the porch. "May I come inside?" he asked with his chin down, but his eyes peering up where she stood at the top of the steps.

Charity shook her head and then coldly answered, "No."

Milton swallowed, taken aback by the icy darts she threw at him. "*Oh* ... well, okay then. You take care of yourself." He then turned around and began walking in the opposite direction.

Charity, realizing her foul attitude and how she wasn't even giving him a chance to say the very words that she had waited so long to hear, suddenly recanted. "But we can sit out here on the porch." She closed the front door behind her and Milton turned around. Charity quietly pulled in a deep breath as he started back towards the porch. As Milton climbed to the top of the steps, she lowered onto one of the white wooden rocking chairs near the large set of double windows that led into Margaret's prided front room.

Milton slowly sat down on the swing bench that was next to Charity and carefully asked, "How have you been?"

"I've been doing okay," she answered, avoiding eye contact as she stared straight ahead.

"Is D.C. treating you all right?"

"It's treating me just fine," she answered in a monot-
onous tone, this time glancing at him before shifting her
eyes away again.

"That's good. The Air Force is treating me all right, I
guess."

Charity appeared uninterested as she crossed her legs
at the ankles.

"I'm still stationed overseas, but I'll be back home
again by next summer. The base here is growing and so
are the opportunities. Have you ever thought about—"

"Just stop it!" Charity blurted as her eyes seemed to
grow twice their size. "What do you want from me?" She
glared in his direction. "To hear me say that I forgive you
for taking my virginity and then leaving me the next day?"

Those words unexpectedly pierced Milton with the
embarrassment Charity felt when he had left.

"Is that what you came here for? For me to forgive
you for acting like you didn't know me in front of your
college friends because I was still in high school at the
time?" As she grilled him, her eyes began to water. "For
calling someone else your girl when I had just given you
something that I could never get back? Well, I can't just
pretend anymore that it was nothing big to me because it
was," Charity cried.

Milton stood and grabbed her by the wrist as she
started for the door. "Charity, wait."

She snatched her arm away. "Just leave me alone!"

"Not until you hear me out." He reached out to her again, grabbing the hem of her sweat suit jacket from behind. "I should have never done that to you. I let my stupid ego get in the way of how I really felt." He tried to wrap his arms around her to no avail. Charity pushed him away, careful to keep her distance. "My mind wasn't where it is now," Milton continued. "I may have been grown, but I definitely wasn't a man."

The tears that streamed from Charity's eyes seemed endless. She had bottled her feelings for so long, hoping that one day they'd just die for him. She didn't want to care for Milton anymore, but her soul was deeply tied to his. Despite her efforts to move on and date others merely to get over him, the connection to Milton stubbornly remained.

"Why did you do it?" She pounded on his chest with the bottom of her fists, hopelessly trying to physically hurt him the way he had hurt her emotionally. "*Why?*" Charity's voice trailed off into nothingness.

Milton pulled her closer and now with little resistance, Charity allowed her head to fall onto his waiting chest. The painful expression etched onto her face painted her soul's struggle. She had to deal with the fact of what her mother had warned her of was indeed the trap she had fallen into: sleeping with a man who said that he loved her, but hadn't proven it by marriage.

"I'm so sorry, baby." Milton engulfed her in his arms, determined to make up the wrong he had done. "It'll never happen again."

Charity struggled to accept his words as the pain was still as fresh today as it was seven years ago. She hadn't realized how deeply she still felt for him until this moment. The hurt had been buried beneath layers of denial, countless moments of regret, and years of unfulfilled relationships.

"No … you're right, it won't ever happen again." Charity smeared her tears with the back of her hand. "You can't just waltz back into my life as if it's that easy for me to let everything go. So, don't you call me baby." Charity pondered her words and then said, "Listen, I do forgive you, but I … I can't trust that you won't just leave again or hurt me as badly as you had in the past."

Milton could sense her love for him beyond her resistance. He was grateful that she was even speaking to him, regardless of how much time had passed. He knew that time didn't heal wounds, especially of this kind, but only God.

It had been two years since he had given his life to Christ and it troubled him every day since then that he had convinced Charity to break the purity pledge she had vowed to God at the age of fifteen. A vow to stay pure until the day she got married. But somewhere in the midst of their relationship, he allowed the ridicule of friends about Charity's age to dictate their relationship.

When she showed up to his going away party the night before he was to leave, he acted as if she was just a friend, not his lady. The moment that hurt the most was when another woman walked up and put her arms around him and he didn't pull away. Charity looked at him with questions pouring from her eyes, but Milton simply allowed her to leave as if they had no personal commitment at all. It wasn't until later around the time Grandma Josie had died that Elisha confided to Milton that many of those very same so-called friends of his had tried to date Charity too.

"And we're different people now. I don't even know who you are anymore." She cautiously moved away from him and paced to the other side of the porch. "I just don't know." She tossed her hands up in the air before folding them across her chest again. "Besides, who was that on the phone?"

Milton shook his head slightly, unsure as to what she was talking about.

"This morning when you were here and walked out of the room to talk," she reminded him.

Milton gently smiled as he said, "*Oh* … that was just my cousin. You remember Sabrina."

"Oh, that was Sabrina? Yeah, I remember her." Charity appeared somewhat relieved, but still withdrawn.

Milton kept the distance Charity had placed between them, but asked her an importantly intimate question, "Do you still love me?"

Charity couldn't bring herself to look into his emotion-filled eyes. It was hard enough to admit it to herself, but it would be an entirely different thing to confess her true feelings to him.

"Charity, I asked you a question. *Do you still love me?*"

She looked away from him, refusing to acknowledge that he had even said anything. It wasn't fair of him to dictate a response of how she felt. It was bad enough that she was challenged with every relationship she had tried to have outside of him, but to admit it would mean that he had the upper hand. Charity stared back into his eyes, wondering if *he* still loved *her*.

"Do you still love me?" Charity turned the question on him.

"Yes, I do," he said without the slightest hesitation.

Unexpectedly, a bashful smile crept across her face that she could not hide. "Then you're going to have to prove it," Charity said matter-of-factly with her hands now propped back onto her hips.

Milton took her hands and stared her deeply in the eyes. "With what I've done to you, I wouldn't have it any other way."

Chapter Five

"Girl, don't be no fool," one of Charity's longtime friends, Yolanda, said before she crammed an appetizer into her mouth.

Charity sighed as she picked at the cucumbers and tomatoes in her garden salad. She had since called Elisha and apologized for not making it to her book fair. Instead, she decided to go out to lunch with some friends she hadn't seen in a while. Since talking with Milton this morning, she still had reservations about meeting him later in the evening.

"Don't listen to her, girl," another one of her high school friends, Renita, chimed in. "We were just kids back then. That was so long ago. But look at him today. He's a college graduate, an officer in the military—"

"*Decorated* officer," Charity corrected with a smile.

Yolanda rolled her eyes and shook her head as she reached for another boneless buffalo wing.

"Yes exactly, a decorated officer. And he's come back home to get the woman he loves." Renita smiled.

Yolanda mimicked a gagging motion with her finger in front of her mouth. "You two are living in la-la land. No man is going to come back for his *supposed* sweetheart," she said with curled lips while her two friends looked on, "to start anything serious while he's traveling the world over." She sucked her teeth. "Get real."

"What are you trying to say, Yolanda, that I'm not good enough?"

"Charity," Yolanda started in a daunting tone, "I have dated plenty of guys in the military and some who work for Fortune 500 companies. And all they want to do is play little childish games. Did it ever occur to you that maybe when we were *kids* back then," she grimaced at Renita, "that all he wanted was a good time? Hence what I said, *games*."

"You can't believe that all guys are like that," Renita challenged her.

"Hmmm, let's see ...." Yolanda stared at the friend they referred to as the black Barbie doll with a soulful voice and said, "What happened to Jason?"

Renita abruptly closed her parted lips.

"Yeah, I thought so." Yolanda smirked and then turned back to Charity. "All I'm saying is to watch yourself. You've saved yourself this long, don't mess up now."

Charity's eyelashes gently fluttered as she took Yolanda's words to heart, remembering that she had been saving herself until Milton.

"Charity, follow your heart," then Renita rolled her eyes at Yolanda, "and not *her* head. If you listen to her, you'll see where it'll get you."

Charity smiled as Yolanda sucked her teeth at Renita again while Renita gave her the hand. They took playful jabs at one another that ended in a good-hearted laugh. The three young women only met when they all traveled home for a visit. This happened to be the weekend of the season. Yolanda was visiting her parents for an extended Thanksgiving holiday since she had settled in Seattle and was scheduled to work through Christmas while Renita drove down a few hours from Alabama, simply because she knew her friends would be in town.

"Where is our food?" Yolanda gaped around the crowded restaurant for their waiter. "They need to hurry up because these wings are about to run out."

"Girl, how do you stay in shape with the way that you eat?" Charity asked Yolanda.

With a proud smile, Yolanda replied, "Good 'ole fashioned exercise and my daddy's good genes." She laughed as Renita and Charity nodded with smiles on their faces.

"That's right, your father was a slim man, but he had a big heart." Charity gently touched Yolanda's hand from across the table, remembering the funeral from three years ago.

"A big heart *and* a firm hand," she mentioned with a giggle. "That man didn't play around when it came to whooping us. My sister and I used to hide under the table when he would try to beat us as kids." Yolanda giggled again as she dipped the last wing in a small cup of ranch dressing. "That's the kind of man I'm holding out for, someone like my dad," she paused, and then added, "minus the firm hand."

All three women busted out laughing. Outings like these really made Charity homesick, but not enough to move back to Lewiston Springs. She was comfortable where she lived and the only thing that would make her consider moving is the husband God chooses for her.

"Well, I told Milton that I'd give him a trial run," Charity said as she slowly stirred her pink lemonade with a clear straw.

"Cee, are you sure?" Yolanda gazed at Charity and then raised an eyebrow at Renita.

"Hey, don't look at me," Renita said. "I think she should go for it. People do change."

Charity nodded, contemplating the opinions posed by both of her friends. She took a sip of her drink and carefully placed the glass back on the table as she said, "I'll give him until Christmas to prove himself ... make him my *Christmas* boyfriend." She intermittently smiled with a sense of confidence. "Yes, that's what I think I'll do."

Chapter Six

Margaret stood in front of her door length mirror, checking herself over one last time before grabbing her Bible from the dresser. After spending the evening alone with her husband, she prepared for worship service at Lewiston Springs Greater Christian Tabernacle.

"Are you almost ready, sweetheart?" Gerald poked his head out from the large walk-in closet with a tie draped around his neck.

"I'm ready, Gerald." She smiled endearingly. "See, I told you that I'd be able to get up this morning."

Gerald nodded as a deep, throaty chuckled rumbled from his mouth. "Yes, yes, you did warn me. Next time, we'll wait until after Sunday morning to celebrate my return home." He flirted with a wink. "But I did have a good time last night."

Margaret modestly smiled, remembering the dinner for two and the private time they shared after hours. It was a welcomed change for her to have Gerald at home after having been gone for over a month. And to now have him through the New Year, she thanked the Lord above for togetherness.

"I did too, honey, but if you don't hurry up and get your shoes on, we're going to be late. We've already missed Sunday School." Margaret slipped her winter coat on that she hadn't needed for the past two days and volunteered to start her vehicle. "I hope the car isn't iced over. That cold snap came out of nowhere."

"You're really ready? You've never finished dressing before me." Gerald smirked as he quickly finagled a knot in his tie. "I guess there's always something new we can learn about one another." He grinned as he sat on the cushioned paisley-print bench at the foot of their king-sized bed and slipped on his comfortable black Stacy Adams shoes.

Margaret didn't reply to his last comment. He was right because there's still a lot more that he has to learn about her. She quickly grabbed her purse from the bed and leaned over to deliver her usual morning kiss. Without another word, she rubbed the color from her lipstick into the darkness of his skin and walked out of the room.

Margaret stopped at the top of the wrought iron staircase and peered into Charity's room where the door was open. She could see that the twin beds were made and wondered if Charity had slept over at Elisha's. She thought it strange because Charity hardly ever got anywhere early so she must've spent the night out. Margaret then shifted her attention to Joy's room where the door was slightly cracked and the lights out also, but she was known for periodically attending the second service that began fifteen minutes after the first one ended on certain Sundays.

Margaret took a moment and peeked inside of Joy's room. She smiled as Joy stirred in her sleep. Careful not to wake her, she backed out and then looked to where her boys used to sleep. Margaret looked forward to having them home soon. It had been a while since she's had her entire family home at one time, especially with Gerald's schedule, but Lord willing December would be one of those months where they could all enjoy each other's company, even if it was only for a day or so.

As Joy coughed in her sleep, Margaret shook from her preoccupation. She straightened her coat, buttoned a few buttons, and then rushed down the stairs out to her car.

Charity sat in the center section of the church with Milton at her side. The two simply looked like they belonged together. Milton's arm was draped behind Charity on the back of the pew bench as her hands rested between the pages of a Bible they both shared. The senior pastor was in the midst of delivering a riveting message about the power of love.

"This Bible," the pastor held the Holy Book up in front of him for effect, "is God's love letter to the world.

From the Old Testament when He created man, all the way to the book of Revelation." He sat the Bible back onto the podium and momentarily peered at it as if in deep thought before saying, "God loves us, saints. We're in the season where we collectively celebrate the Savior's birth ... that's what Christmas is truly about. When Jesus explained to us why He was sent to earth in John 3:16, He didn't do it because we were righteous, He didn't do it to condemn us, He did it because of love."

The congregants nodded in agreement while others said amen.

"I wonder if we all even know what the *true* meaning of love is," the pastor lamented. "Love is not envious or prideful. It's not resentful or self-seeking. It's not vain or rude. Do you hear me, Church?"

Again, the congregants replied with sentiments of approval.

"So, what is love?" the pastor rhetorically asked as he paced from behind the pulpit. "Love is transparent, open to admitting when you've done wrong."

Charity then gazed at Milton who at that moment inched closer to her.

"But also remember that God's Word tells us that love, *true* love, keeps no record of those wrong doings," the pastor continued. "You know, many people throw around that word love like it's nothing. People say they love their cars, or they love their clothes, or even that they love their homes." He then donned a serious glare. "Jesus didn't die for materialistic things; He died for you and for me." The compelling preacher then grinned as he said, "I don't know about you, but I'm not about to put myself in the same category as a new blouse or pair of expensive shoes." Some congregants chuckled, but then the pastor fell serious again as he added, "And neither should you."

Milton clutched Charity's hand and gave it a light squeeze just as he had on last night when they parted ways. He wanted to kiss her, but she wouldn't let him and he understood. Milton knew that Charity wasn't keeping a record of his wrong-doing, but simply protecting her feelings. They had spent hours talking after he took her out for dinner at her favorite restaurant and a night walk on the pier. It was reminiscent of the date that led up to Charity giving herself to him; the intimate moment that her best friends Yolanda and Renita knew nothing about. Charity had justified in her mind that she and Milton would be married one day, but never considered the possibility of their relationship ending, especially the way that it had.

Margaret discreetly peered at her daughter from the section of seating where the ministers' wives usually sat. With this being Gerald's first Sunday back home, he chose to sit with his wife instead of in the pulpit with the other associate ministers.

"Looks like the Lord has everything worked out between them," Gerald whispered to Margaret, trying to pull her attention back to the Word of God. "He's obviously forgiven all that's been said." He referred to the terrible argument they had with Laurence and Francine years ago.

"It sure looks that way," she responded, giving Gerald a pacifying smile. Margaret then quietly sighed as her eyes searched the sanctuary for any signs of Laurence and Francine. Kim was seated a few rows from the back. Margaret had seen her enter with another woman before service began, but her parents were nowhere to be found. Margaret settled into her seat, trying to wrap her mind around Francine's true absence yesterday, but as the Holy Spirit tugged at her heart, she decided to give her full attention to the message that began to speak clearly to her heart.

"Love is truth and honesty that never fails." The pastor then stepped down to the floor with the microphone in hand. "God *is* love," he passionately informed. "You can come to the Lord with whatever problem or situation you may have. God is not like man who holds onto every single thing that you've done. His love isn't conditional." The pastor paused before he said, "So don't be afraid to admit your faults. The Bible tells us that no matter what we've done, we can ask for forgiveness and that He is faithful and just to forgive us."

As the pastor drew his sermon to a close, he summoned forth those who desired prayer. It was an altar call for anyone who needed to release burdens that heavily weighed them down. It pierced the hearts of many who shuffled their way to the front of the church. And also without hesitation, Margaret quickly moved out of her row and made her way to the altar.

Gerald looked on, wondering what was bothering his wife. She hadn't shared anything with him that would warrant her to move with such urgency. Moreover, they had prayed a moving prayer to the Lord just hours before. Unaware of what could be troubling his wife, Gerald followed her to the altar and stood supportively at her side.

Chapter Seven

Laurence sat in his vehicle, having arrived just moments before Sunday morning's second worship service was set to begin. He thought back to his wife whom he had left in bed. Although Francine was under the weather, he doubted that she would've come to the brunch Margaret held yesterday and even wearier of her attendance at church today. She had been missing several Sundays here and there although she claimed to have gotten past the argument she had with Margaret.

"I've got to stop doing that," Laurence said to himself. His desire to have the relationship with Francine that Gerald had with Margaret was leading his mind astray. He and Margaret's relationship was an innocent friendship, but on yesterday he temporarily found himself envisioning more. His wife wasn't up to coming to church, but this was something he had to pray off of him with or without her. He knew it was only a fleeting emotion that really wasn't about Margaret, but about the hole of loneliness he felt every time Francine refused to accompany him at certain functions.

Laurence sighed to himself as he got out of his vehicle dressed in a sharp blue suit and tie. Despite the bone-chilling weather, he walked towards the entrance with his trench coat draped across his right arm. Laurence looked back momentarily to activate his car alarm before hustling up the walkway.

"Oh my goodness," Margaret gasped as she turned around. "I didn't see you there." With a gentle smile she backed away from Laurence. "Are you headed into the second service?"

Laurence cleared his throat and smiled. "Yes, I am. Francine still wasn't feeling well, so I spent a little time with her this morning."

"Laurence, how are you doing this morning?" Gerald interrupted as he walked up behind his wife. He reached around her to give Laurence a firm handshake.

"I'm good, just trying to get used to this iffy weather." Laurence lightheartedly chuckled, and then said, "It kept my wife home this morning."

"Oh, we're sorry to hear that," Gerald said with a downcast expression. "Is she still not feeling well?"

Laurence rubbed his bare hands together as he carefully answered, "It appears that way."

"I tell you, it sure is hard to tell the seasons apart nowadays." Gerald shook his head.

"So true," Laurence agreed as Gerald draped his arm around Margaret's shoulders. "Some days the winter months are almost like spring." Laurence shifted his eyes towards the double doors where congregants were piling in and out of the sanctuary.

"Well, we don't want to keep you," Margaret spoke up. "And please tell Francine again that we asked about her."

"I will," Laurence answered as Gerald shook his hand again. "You two have a good afternoon."

"Thank you and you do the same," Gerald replied as Margaret simply waved.

Laurence stared at Margaret as she and Gerald walked away, remembering the amicable friendship they all shared at one time. At that moment in relief, that's all he felt, particularly for Margaret—was a friendship. He just wanted that intimacy back with his wife that had somehow drifted away. He looked up towards the sky and smiled, he knew God was going to work it out ... somehow. With a quick double-check in his coat pocket for his wallet, Laurence hurried inside of the church.

Charity sat inside of Milton's rental and stared at her parents walking towards the parking lot. She looked down at her lap and fidgeted with the pen in her hand, wondering why Mayor Grayson had gazed at her parents the way that he had. She then glanced over at Milton who was standing at the front of the car talking with an old friend. Charity waited patiently, hoping that he had another reminiscent day planned for them.

"Are you ready to go?" Milton asked as he sat behind the steering wheel and stared in her direction.

"Yeah, I'm ready."

"Did you want to go home for a change of clothes?"

Charity shook her head. "No, just take me by Elisha's. I left some extra clothes there from last night. And thanks for driving over and picking me up this morning."

Milton gazed at her lovingly. "Now you know that you don't have to thank me for that."

Charity gently smiled as she strapped on her seatbelt. "Well, I know. I just wanted you to know that I'm taking notice of what you're trying to do." She thought back to the girl chat she had with Renita and Yolanda.

"Is it working?" Milton asked with a grin.

"Let's just say that I had a really nice time on yesterday," Charity admitted, slowly allowing her protective guard down.

"I'm glad because the best is yet to come."

"We'll see about that," she said with a smirk.

Milton returned a million dollar smile as he started the engine and drove out of the parking lot.

Chapter Eight

"We're going to need more props over here," the musical play director called out to several assistants who were volunteering their time for the Christmas gala.

Charity stood off to the side with Milton as they went over a few lines for the scene they were rehearsing. "I sure hope we have a good turnout. Mama has worked really hard pulling everything together."

"Well, with it being in the newspaper and all over Facebook, I'm sure that there'll be a crowd." Milton smiled. "Besides, my classmates can't wait to see me act. They love a joke."

Charity giggled as she looked back down at the script. "I'm sure it'll be fine."

Milton stared at her in amazement, wondering why he ever risked losing her. That other woman wasn't worth losing her over, in hindsight, no woman would have been worth losing Charity. There was a solid connection between them that he couldn't put into words, but it came to life every time they saw each other. The past two weeks was like meeting each other for the first time all over again.

"Are you guys ready to rehearse this scene again?" the assertive director questioned. "Good job, Milton. This time we need you to do it with more feeling, Charity."

Charity placed a hand on her hip as Marshall, the director, strutted away to gather a few other actors for the scene. "What is he talking about? I did do it with feeling."

"I think what he means is that you seem a little stand-offish." Milton chuckled. "You're supposed to be my leading lady and we're supposed to be in love."

Charity shook her head in annoyance as her eyes rolled from Milton back to Marshall who was now thumbing through a stack of papers. "Whatever." She nonchalantly tossed the script onto a folding chair. "I've got this."

Milton followed her lead and they took their marks.

It was as if a complete transformation took place. The performance Charity delivered was sure to receive a standing ovation. Not once did she have to rely on the script, showing that her mother was right in picking her because of how quickly she memorized lines. With one week left until show time, Charity proved that she'd be ready. They only had one more scene to rehearse before doing a complete run-through of all the lines. Milton's lines were as smooth as hers until his eyes met with an unexpected pair in the audience.

"Milton, it's your line," Charity whispered. *"You're right, Christmas is more than shopping at the mall or getting the latest gadget on sale...,"* she tried to remind him.

Milton stalled before snapping his attention away from Anita who watched the rehearsal from an auditorium seat with other patrons who were seated sparsely throughout the theater.

"Okay, let's stop here," Marshall instructed. "It's getting late anyway. We'll redo this scene tomorrow everybody and then start on the next one." He then looked to Milton. "Take your script home. I thought you had it." Marshall shook his head, but then smiled at Charity. "You were perfect. See you guys tomorrow night."

Charity laughed as Marshall and the others gathered their things and walked off stage. "And to think he was just singing your praises."

Milton half-heartedly smiled as he peered out to the auditorium seating again. Anita was gone. Only Joy and her friend, Michelle, remained who were now putting on their coats.

"What is it?" Charity's grin was hampered by Milton's lack of humor. Her eyes followed his to the empty theater seating with the exception of Joy and Michelle who were now walking down one of the aisles in their direction.

"It's nothing." Milton regained eye contact with Charity and shook his head. "Uh, did you still want to catch a movie?"

Charity shrugged as she glanced at her watch. "I guess so. It's still early enough."

"Hey Charity, I'm about to drop Michelle off at home," Joy said as she walked up the steps to the stage. "Are you going home or spending the night at Elisha's?"

Charity slid her eyes away from Joy and coyly smiled at Milton as she answered, "I'm going home tonight. I think we kept Elisha up too late the last time I slept over. She has to work in the morning."

"Okay, love birds," Joy teased and turned away from her sister to Milton. "Can you at least let me spend one day with my sister before she leaves?"

Milton grinned as Charity playfully pushed Joy's arm.

"Girl stop, we have not been spending *that* much time together."

"Whatever." Joy giggled and then glanced at Michelle before pulling her cell from the front pocket of her thick, hooded sweater. "If that's true, then I guess I'll see you later."

Charity nudged her sister again. "You'll see me, I promise. You can show me pictures from your pageant."

"All right, Cee." Joy smiled at Charity as she started for the side door exit. "I'll be over at Michelle's for a little bit, so tell Mama."

"I will." Charity grinned, watching as Joy and Michelle waved on their way out the door.

"Your little sister is a trip," Milton said.

"Tell me about it. She is something."

"So, are you ready to go? We can just grab something to eat instead of seeing a movie," Milton suggested. "I don't want Commander Joy reprimanding me again," he said, successfully soliciting laughter from Charity.

"Yeah, we better because I'll never hear the end of it."

♥ ♥ ♥

A waiter at *Maurice's*, a quaint bistro nestled in the center of town, shamelessly asked to have his picture taken with Milton. Charity softly smiled as the man insisted on a photo with the hometown hero who had received a purple heart for his sacrifice in the Armed Services. There was even a photograph of him on the wall alongside other well-known veterans who had served the country during different war periods. Milton was the first out the group to have received a purple heart and lived to tell about it.

"My father was in the Army and my grandfather was in the Navy," the waiter excitedly said. "It is such an honor to meet you. I just want to personally say thank you."

The corners of Milton's mouth modestly rose. "Well, I was just doing my part. I appreciate your kind words, but just give thanks to God."

Those words caused Charity's heart to melt. To hear Milton openly praise God confirmed for her that he had really changed. She lowered her head as they continued to talk, pretending to look for a dish on the menu, but all she could think about was how much she had never stopped loving him. Her eyes misted as true forgiveness conquered her fears. It was just as the Scripture stated in 1 John 4:18: *There is no fear in love; but perfect love casts out fear, because fear involves torment. But he who fears has not been made perfect in love. Perfect love casts out all fear.*

"I'm sorry ma'am. I didn't mean to hold you all up, but I had to get a picture with Mr. Grayson," the waiter apologized. "I've always wanted to go in the military, but this bum leg of mine wouldn't allow it."

"Oh, just call me Milton. And I'm sure my date doesn't mind," he said, casually reaching for Charity's left hand.

With her right hand, Charity gently brushed locks of her hair back from her eyes, having successfully stifled her tears. "Oh no, I'm fine." She slowly moved her other hand away from Milton's before burying her face back into the menu.

"Have you decided what you're going to have, ma'am?" The waiter pulled a pen and notepad from his red waist apron.

"Uh, not really." She looked back up at him. "Can we have a moment?"

"Sure, no problem." The neatly dressed man in a pair of black pants, a white collared shirt, and a red tie tucked his pen and notepad back into his pocket. He then turned the long stemmed glasses from the table right side up. "How about I pour you both a couple glasses of water until you decide?"

Charity seemed distracted so Milton motioned for the waiter to leave them alone.

"Is everything okay?" Milton asked in concern. His piercing brown eyes steadied onto hers.

Charity waved her hand as she suddenly started chuckling. Milton raised an eyebrow.

"I'm fine," she started, "I was just thinking about our first date. Do you remember when we got caught in the rain?"

Milton jerked his head back as a nostalgic glow surfaced on his face. "Yes, how could I forget? The wind was so hard that day that my umbrella blew inside out."

Charity laughed, recalling how soaked she had gotten. Not only had she looked like a raccoon around the eyes from the smeared mascara, but her then relaxed hair clung to her face like plastic wrap.

"It's good to hear you laugh," Milton said in between his chuckles. "I remember that day very clearly."

"So do I. That's one of the reasons why I decided to just go natural. The wetter my hair gets now, the better it looks."

They both chuckled.

"Well, if I haven't told you already, it looks really good on you," Milton complimented.

"Thank you." Charity blushed. "I still wear it straight every now and then." She stared back down at the menu.

Moments later, the waiter returned to the table with a maroon linen cloth covered basket of buttered rolls and a pitcher of water. He poured iced water into the two glasses already placed in front of Milton and Charity and then took their orders.

"Would either of you like a garden salad to go with your meals?"

Milton and Charity stared at one another and both shook their heads.

"Okay, I'll go ahead and put your orders in." The waiter reached for the menus that were on the table beside a seasonal poinsettia plant and slid them underneath his arm. "If you need anything else, my name is Victor," he politely added before walking back towards the kitchen.

"I have something for you." Milton slipped his hand inside of his coat pocket and pulled out a beautiful heart-shaped gold locket.

Charity took the locket in her hands and peered down at the date of her purity pledge engraved on the back. "Where did you get this?" She slowly gazed up at him.

"I found it outside on the ground at my parents' house. You must've dropped it the night you left my going away party."

Charity's jaw tightened.

"I didn't see it until the next morning when I was leaving."

"Why didn't you tell me?"

Milton looked at her apologetically. "Charity, I tried to before I left, but you weren't trying to hear anything that I had to say." He then paused before he added, "And I don't blame you."

She resignedly sighed. "You could have left it with Elisha. This means a lot to me."

"And *you* mean a lot to me." Milton slid his hands across the table again and held onto Charity's. "I didn't want to send this with Elisha. It was special to me too. It was intimate ... it was private. I never told anyone what happened between us. *Never.*"

Charity knew that it would have broken her father's heart. She was close to him and unlike most girls she knew, Charity shared just about everything with her dad. The things she couldn't or wouldn't go to her mother about with the exception of when he was out of town and not to be disturbed.

"But why are you just giving this to me? We've been seeing each other for weeks now."

"Because I wanted to wait until you trusted me. I was never going to keep it. I just wanted to wait until the time was right." Milton softly smiled. "How would you have reacted if I gave this to you that day on the porch … that first day we had seen each other in years?"

Charity sighed, but didn't say anything immediately.

"I just wanted to give it to you after we've had a chance to talk, to settle things from before."

"Milton, I …." Charity stifled her words as the waiter returned with their dinner. She quietly cleared her throat as the plates were placed before them.

"You two enjoy your dinner," Victor kindly said, and then walked away again.

"Did you want to pray?" Milton asked.

Charity modestly motioned to him. "You can." She then lowered her head, waiting to hear him do something she'd never witnessed.

His prayer sounded as if he really had a personal relationship with Jesus Christ. Not only did Milton pray over the food, but he also prayed about their broken relationship. Charity looked up at Milton, but his eyes were still closed. She listened as he continued to petition God to bring them closer together in perfect love.

Charity pondered on how she willingly released her inhibitions with Milton in what seems like only last night. Something so beautiful, so sacred was marred by the way it happened. If she had just waited until he came back for her, like he said he would. If she had just called his what seems like a bluff in hindsight, would that had made him faithful? Did she give in too soon? All of these questions relentlessly rattled around in her head even after Milton had ended the prayer by saying, "Amen."

"Excuse me," Charity abruptly said as she pulled the linen napkin from her lap and hurried to the back of the restaurant where the restrooms were.

Milton looked on with a fork dangling from his fingers. He folded in his lips and dropped the utensil onto his plate while shaking his head from side to side. *"Lord, am I going about things the right way to win her back?"* Milton whispered to God. He didn't want to push too hard, but he also didn't want to let Charity slip away again.

"Sir, how's the food?" Victor stopped back by the table. "Did you need anything?" he questioned, momentarily glancing at the empty seat across from Milton.

"The food is good, thank you." Milton picked up a roll and broke off a piece. "And no we don't need anything right now. We're good."

Victor nodded with a smile and walked to another table a few feet away.

Milton took a bite of the roll and sparingly sipped from his glass of water. He sighed to himself as he peered towards the back of the restaurant where Charity had disappeared. He rubbed his fingertips together and poppy seeds from the bread fell onto the table. Milton then reached into his coat pocket that was on the seat next to him. As he searched the second pocket for his phone when the first one he tried came up empty, Milton glanced to the outside. By happenstance while holding his cell in the palm of his hand, Milton's eyes ran across Anita again. *"What is she doing here?"* he mumbled to himself.

Anita was seated in a coffee shop across the street with a cup in her hand. Milton looked closer as his eyes shifted from her to the woman seated across from her. Suddenly, a wave of curiosity floated over him.

"I'm sorry. I just needed a moment," Charity apologized, splitting Milton's attention as she sat back down. "So, how's your food?"

"It's good." Milton tore his eyes away from Anita and peered into Charity's eyes.

"What is it?" she asked, looking in the direction Milton had just turned his attention away from. "Is that Mama?" She squinted. "I thought she had a meeting to go to tonight." Charity pulled her plate of food closer as she placed the linen napkin she had tossed aside earlier back onto her lap. "I wonder who that woman is she's with. If she's still there when we're finished eating, we can stop in and say hello."

Milton hesitantly nodded, and then began picking at his food.

Charity took notice of his peculiar behavior and asked, "I thought you said that the food was good." She then smiled, having left her insecurities behind.

"Oh, it is." Milton tried to recover from his distraction. "I'm just not as hungry as I thought I was."

"Well, eating those rolls can do that to a person," Charity grinned, pointing at the broken piece of bread on his plate. "That's how they get you to think that you've had a big meal at a reasonable price. *Everybody* leaves full." She laughed, completely opposite from the shaken woman who had rushed off only moments ago.

"I think you're right about that," Milton said as he glanced back to where Margaret and Anita were seated. "They're gone," he gasped.

Charity glanced across the street and saw that her mother was no longer in the locally owned coffee shop she had always raved about. "Oh wow, that was fast," she said, searching the sidewalks nearby. "That must've been somebody else working on things for the gala."

"Oh, does she have a lot of people working behind the scenes?" Milton curiously questioned.

"Well, I wouldn't say a lot, but over the past few days I've heard several people call the house that I've never met." Charity broke off a piece of bread for herself. "And Mama does not give the house number out to too many people." She giggled.

Milton dabbed the corners of his mouth with a napkin before taking another sip from his glass of water. He swallowed slowly before setting his drink back on the table.

"Is everything all right?" Charity inquired, struggling to gain eye contact with Milton.

"I'm good," he said in an attempt to convince her. "I'm just happy to be here with you."

"Milton, I am too." Charity bashfully twirled her fork into her spaghetti. "Over the past couple of weeks, I've seen things in you that I have never seen before. Things that I really like."

Milton tilted his head to one side. "Like what?"

"Well, for starters, you're saved now."

Milton nodded. "Yeah, I had to do it. I guess you can say when you're faced with a life or death situation, it kind of makes you see things more clearly." He offhandedly chuckled. "But seriously, I was scared when that plane went down. I could have lost my life and my soul. So, I decided to do what our pastor had been saying for years, give my life to Christ."

Charity smiled, softened at the spiritual change in him. "Yeah, that's so important. I guess for me it was just a matter of living the life of a Christian."

"What do you mean?" Milton inquired before he took a small bite of his food.

"Well, it took me a while to get past breaking my vow to God." She nervously glanced down.

"Charity, I'm sorry—"

She held up a hand to silence him. "No, it's not your fault. I'm coming to realize that now. We weren't married and you did not rape me. I made the decision to…" Her words trailed thin as she watched a couple walk past them to the exit. "Well, you know."

"Yeah, but things could've been different. I could've been a little bit stronger …" His words then diminished into nothing.

They both looked at each other and smiled.

"Did you want to get this food to go?" Milton asked. "I think we really need to talk," he looked around as the traffic picked up in the bistro, "and this is not the place to do it."

Charity couldn't agree with him more.

After getting their food boxed in takeout containers, Milton escorted Charity out to the car. He opened the door for her and placed the containers on the backseat. On their drive home, Milton confided that the woman they saw seated across from Margaret was the same woman that he had left her for. Although his relationship with Anita didn't last long after he had left for Basic Training, he knew that time didn't matter to Charity. The fact that he had convinced her to give in to him shattered the trust they had developed. That was until now.

"Are you sure that was her? When was the last time you saw her?" Charity challenged him. "And how would she know my mother?"

"I don't know how she knows your mother," Milton started, "and I promise you, I haven't seen her in years … but I'm sure that's her. Just before we left rehearsal, I saw her in the audience watching us practice."

Charity slowly shook her head. "Why didn't you say anything?"

Milton pulled into her parents' driveway and parked the car. "Because when I looked again, she was gone. And I figured that maybe I was mistaken until I saw her again talking to your mother." Milton aimed to be as transparent as possible, leaving nothing to break the trust Charity was developing in him.

"That's strange. I wonder how she knows my mother." Charity took off her seatbelt and reached for the door handle.

"I wanted to be upfront with you, Charity. I really want us back."

Charity smiled softly, although somewhat distracted by what he had just shared with her.

"I'm not saying this just to hear myself talk, I really mean it. I want us to be together." Milton wore his heart on his sleeve and Charity took notice. "But I don't want to force you to be with me."

When he said those words Charity felt his sincerity. She watched closely as Milton sighed and looked straight ahead. Something inside of her moved, erasing the residual doubt she had about him. Milton's candor stirred the love she still had inside for him. He was telling her the truth. Charity knew now that she could trust him and that's all she had ever wanted, a man that was faithful to God and truthful to her. And over the past few years of trying to find substitutes for her soulmate where there weren't any, God had now blessed her with the real thing.

"Milton, I know that we're not perfect and I've given you a bit of a hard time lately," she paused with a grin, "but I do love you. I *still* love you."

In a timid voice, Milton said, "I love you too, babe." Still wanting Charity to be secure in her decision, Milton reserved any physical contact. After learning, truly understanding, the delicate nature of a saved woman, he regretted having put her in such a position years prior.

Charity placed a hand on his cheek and gently pulled his face towards her. She closed her eyes and remembered their first kiss all over again. The gentleness of Milton's touch caressed her heart. Despite all that had happened between them, she knew that he was the one. He had always been the one.

Chapter Nine

"Hey, I'm glad I caught you," Kim said to her older brother as she met him outside of their parents' home. "Do you mind checking in on my dog while I'm gone? Mama is volunteering at the homeless shelter this week and you know Daddy, he's busy with the city."

Milton grimaced and rearranged her words as a question, "*Check in on your dog?* Where are you going?"

"I have to go out of town for my job. Last minute trip just a few counties over." She slid a spare key into his hand.

"Hey, I didn't say yes."

"*Please,*" Kim pleaded. "I can't take him with me and this could mean that promotion I've been hoping for." Kim then put her hands in a praying position. "Come on, Milton. I've looked out for you on several occasions." She asked the request again with the motions of her eyes and then tested him by questioning, "*What would Jesus do?*"

Milton laughed at his sister and answered, "Tell you to not use Him as a ploy." Ever since he shared with his family that he had gotten saved over a year and a half ago, they used it to their advantage by calling in favors they knew he normally would not do.

"*Please*," Kim repeated, peering at him with her big, brown eyes.

Still softened by how his date went with Charity, Milton was in the hospitable mood. "I guess so."

"Oh, thank you!" Kim pecked him on the cheek, and then she rattled off care instructions for her pet Chihuahua. "I'll be back the day after tomorrow."

"You better be."

"I will, I promise." And as if to sweeten the pot she cleverly added, "I just went grocery shopping and have chocolate chip cookies in the pantry and vanilla ice cream in the freezer." Kim knew that was his favorite combination for a delectable dessert.

"Yeah, thanks." Milton slyly grinned.

"Okay, I leave in the morning, so she'll be fine until around noon. But please sleep over, she hates being alone at night."

Milton shook his head at Kim and grunted. "You just better be back the next morning or your little pooch is going to be riding solo."

"I will," Kim said as she hurried to her car parked in front of the house. "Thanks again!" she yelled out to him as she drove off into the night.

"What did I just get myself into?" Milton asked himself as he walked up the walkway, jiggling his keys in his front pocket.

Milton walked inside his parents' house and heard loud voices upstairs. The lights were out on the first floor with the exception of a glow coming from a plug-in flash light in the hallway. Milton closed the door and placed the keys on a table in the foyer before starting upstairs.

"Fran, let bygones be bygones." Laurence sighed. "She organized a wonderful brunch for my unofficial campaign meeting and was even there at the press conference when I officially announced it to the public. Can we just move forward?"

Francine unfolded her crossed arms and paced to the other side of the bedroom. "How can you just let it go? She's never apologized to me," she huffed. "But I'm supposed to just go about my business and sit up in her house eating *brunch* while she plays Clair Huxtable." Francine sighed as she picked up her golden colored mug and sipped sparingly. "I remember what she said about my son." She snappily groaned.

Milton leaned his ear closer to the slightly cracked door of his parents' bedroom, careful to remain quiet.

"That's the problem, Fran, you *remember* everything," Laurence criticized. "What about what you said?"

"Are you defending her now?" Francine's eyes grew as she buried them into Laurence. "Need I remind you that Milton is your son too?"

"Him being my son does not excuse the way he treated their daughter. You saw how Charity looked when she would come to church and how she became less and less involved in the youth ministry around that time." Laurence loosened his necktie. "When I saw her, I thought about Kim. I don't know what I would've have said or how I would've reacted. It was probably a good thing that Gerald was out of town during that time."

Francine seemed to be taking Laurence's words to heart. She placed the mug back on the nightstand from where she had retrieved it only moments ago and plopped down on the foot of their bed, avoiding eye contact with her husband. She knew he was right and the anger she held against Margaret hindered her worship to God.

"And you know how Milton was back then." Laurence delivered a telling eye once he regained eye contact with his wife. "I wouldn't say that he was a Casanova, but I knew my son. Charity was a good girl and Margaret just wanted there to be peace between our families. Is there something wrong with that?"

Milton grimly folded in his lips as he backed away from their door. He knew that his reputation from the past was garbage as far as the ladies were concerned, but he was different now. Milton eased away from his parents' bedroom door and walked to his old bedroom. He quickly packed a duffel bag, not wanting to stick around to hear another word.

After stuffing his bag for a couple of nights stay at Kim's, Milton eased back down the stairs and out the front door without his parents knowing he had ever been there. Once behind the steering wheel, he sighed in regret. He wondered if it would just be better if he left Charity alone. Maybe then there would be peace between the families and people would stop talking behind his back, especially his parents and the parents of the woman he loved.

Seriously contemplating whether or not it was such a good idea to pursue Charity any further, Milton backed out of the driveway and drove to his sister's place.

Charity walked through the front door still high on Milton. She felt free to love again. No longer was she enamored with the cumbersome notion that she was meant to live with what he had done because she finally realized that there was nothing she could do to change what had already happened. Charity came to terms with knowing no matter how many times she had cried herself to sleep over Milton, God held her future and He is where she had to put her complete trust.

"Daddy, are you here?" Charity called out, but didn't get an answer. Since she had entered through the front door, Charity walked to the garage and called out again, "Daddy?"

Charity's eyes scanned the vacant garage floor with the exception of the family SUV. Joy's car was gone whom she expected to be home soon, but her father's pick-up truck was absent as well. Charity assumed that he was either out at a hardware store purchasing items for a new project or visiting a few sick church members that he was commonly known for doing. With a soft smile on her face, Charity closed the door to the garage that led into the house.

Charity gasped as she met eyes with Margaret who had just come through the kitchen door. "*Oh Mama*, I didn't know you were home."

Margaret playfully held her hands up. "I'm sorry, didn't mean to scare you."

Charity giggled as she held her chest. "I'm okay. It was just so quiet that I didn't think anyone was home. Your car wasn't out front or in the garage."

"Oh, I just got home just now."

"I didn't hear you drive up."

"Well, I drove around back since Gerald wants to wash my car tomorrow." Margaret grinned as she cleansed her hands at the sink. "You know your father, he wants to always stay busy. I told him that I could have somebody do that, but he recited his favorite line '*why pay somebody to do something that I can do myself.*'" Margaret reached into the cupboard for a glass. "So, I'll be driving the SUV on tomorrow." She tugged on the refrigerator door handle and retrieved a pitcher of lemonade. "Would you like some?" Margaret asked as she poured a drink for herself.

"Oh, no thank you. I'm fine." Charity leaned against the counter where her mother stood. She fidgeted with her fingernails, trying to figure out how to ask her mother how she knew Anita.

"What is it? Something is bothering you." Margaret casually took a sip from her glass. "And please stand up straight," she instructed, moving locks of Charity's hair from her eyes.

Charity pushed her mother's hand away as she walked towards a barstool. "Mama, how do you know that woman you were talking to tonight?"

Margaret momentarily held the glass of lemonade in front of her face before slowly placing it onto the counter.

"Milton and I went out to dinner tonight and we saw you across the street at the coffee shop." Charity glanced down as she repeated her question, "How do you know that woman?"

Margaret sighed as she walked to the table on the other side of the room. Her eyes met with Charity's again as she lowered her body onto a chair. "I knew this was going to come out sooner or later."

Charity moved closer to Margaret as she folded her arms. "What are you talking about?"

"Sit down, Charity. I have something to tell you."

Charity obeyed her mother's instruction and sat down next to her. Margaret looked upwards, praying to God for strength. Her prayer that Sunday at church when she rushed to the altar was that her daughter would understand her actions from years ago. Margaret had justified that she was only doing what was best for her family and her career.

"Mama, what is it?" Charity's attentive eyes blinked in concern.

"Charity, that was the woman who Milton left you for when he went in the military. Her name is Anita."

Charity twiddled her thumbs as she responded, "I know that now. Milton told me when we saw you two together."

"I see." Margaret nervously wet her lips. "How are things between you two? Are you two back together?"

Charity smiled as she said, "I guess you can say that. We've worked everything out."

"I'm glad."

"I know that's what you were trying to do." Charity playfully nudged her mother's hand. "And thank you."

Margaret nodded peaceably. "I've always wanted what was best for you."

"And you think that's Milton, even after what he's done?"

Margaret nodded. "Now I do. I've been able to see him grow into a respectable young man. But I must admit that I didn't want you two together because of his age and the reputation he had, and neither did your father, but things are much different now."

"Yes, things are different now." Charity pulled in a deep breath, still harboring the secret that she had slept with Milton. She hated to admit it to herself, but her mother had been right about him. "Things are very different now. He's saved, Mama." Charity felt good sharing her heart with Margaret. It seemed as if this visit home welcomed good changes between them as well.

"Laurence told me a while ago," Margaret confided. "I think it was around the time he was wounded in the line of duty."

Baffled, Charity questioned, "Mayor Grayson shared that with you? So, why didn't you ever say anything?"

Margaret shrugged. "I guess because you always told me that you didn't want to talk about him."

"Mama, since when have you ever listened to what I said?" Charity giggled.

"Well, this was different. I saw how you were when he left and the relationships you had afterwards—"

"Oh don't remind me," Charity droned.

The two women cackled as if they were longtime friends. Margaret gazed at her daughter and saw so much of her at that age, an entrepreneur at heart. The difference between them was that Charity lived life for Charity and not for anyone's approval.

As Margaret chatted with her daughter, she reminisced. It had always been her dream to open an event planning and decorating business, but her mother would have never entertained such an idea. She was going to be the city's first black female District Attorney and not some run-of-the-mill planner, as Josie Henderson would always refer. "Be practical, be level-headed," her deceased mother would always say. And if it meant sacrificing a meal here and there while working three jobs for her daughter to get there, then so be it. Receiving a top-notch education was on Josie's list of priorities for Margaret's life, second only to being saved.

"Mama, you know, it's so good talking with you like this. I guess it took me moving away and building a life for myself," Charity admitted with a playful smirk. "But I meant what I told you. I'm going to pay you back the money for my student loan."

Margaret grinned at her daughter. "That was just to teach you a lesson about responsibility. You know that Gerald would have just given you the money, but I wanted to instill in you what my mother had in me."

"But Mama, I'm not you."

"I'm beginning to see that now."

Charity smiled as she stood from the table and started in the opposite direction. She stopped short of the door and turned back to Margaret. "Oh, what were you going to say? I interrupted you earlier. Something about how you know that woman I saw you with tonight."

It was as if a dark cloud had hovered over Margaret. The beautiful conversation they just had was quickly overshadowed by what she had promised God she'd tell her daughter. Margaret had confided in Gerald days before and he prayed with and for his wife. As she cried on his shoulder that night after attending worship service, Gerald reminded Margaret that he married her for better or for worse.

"Mama, what is it?" Charity snapped Margaret from her daze.

Margaret gazed at her daughter and said, "I never meant for you to get hurt."

Charity's nose crinkled as she frowned. "What are you talking about?"

Margaret walked over to where Charity stood and explained, "Anita worked as an intern in the county office. She was in her last year of college and trying to make ends meet. Well, I guess like many broke college students."

"Okay, so she was just meeting with you to get an old job back or something?"

"No, she was meeting to ask me for some money," Margaret regretfully admitted.

"Money ... why?"

"Well, because I had given her money before."

"*Why*?" Charity gasped.

Margaret folded her arms as she meandered over to the window. "I'm not proud of this, but I was just trying to get you to take off those rose colored glasses you looked at Milton through. But when you came home crying that night—"

"How did you know that I was crying?"

"Charity, I heard you in your room. I heard you on the phone with Elisha." Margaret pensively sighed. "It broke my heart that he had broken yours. Although I didn't want you two together at the time, nothing in me wanted you to go through that."

"Mama—"

Margaret held a finger up. "Let me finish. I've started this and I have to finish." She then took a deep breath. "When I told Laurence and Francine that their son wasn't good enough for you, Francine went off. But I guess she had every right to. She told me that I was a high sadistic creature who thought the world revolved around me."

"She said that?" Charity searched Margaret's eyes as if expecting a different answer.

Margaret nodded. "Yes, she did, but what I said about her son was worse. I told her to keep her son on a leash and dogs like him shouldn't be allowed to roam the streets. And maybe the apple didn't fall too far from the tree."

"*Mama*, how could you?"

"Don't run to her defense, it wasn't like she was up there praising you either."

"I can't believe this." Charity propped her hands on her hips and shook her head. "Is there anything else I should know?"

"Well ..." Margaret stalled before she blurted out, "he fell for the bait."

Charity narrowed her eyes as she sought clarity. "What bait?"

Margaret sighed. "I wanted to tell you this a long time ago, but after seeing how hurt you were, I didn't think you'd understand."

"Mama, what are you talking about?" Charity probed.

"I paid Anita to lure Milton away from you."

Charity's eyes pierced her mother's as she questioned, "*You did what?*"

"It was the only way to get you to see who he really was. That man wasn't trying to settle down with anybody and I wanted better for you. I wanted you to go out and experience the world instead of settling—"

"*Settling?* I was not settling!" Charity shook her head in disbelief. "Mama, how could you? *Why* ... why would you do something like that?"

"I wasn't trying to hurt you," Margaret tried to explain. "I was trying to get you to see where his head was at the time. Believe me, I wish I had never done that. I can see that he's a changed person, but you've got to remember that I was not the one who left you."

"But Mama, don't you understand? *You* were the one who set it up," Charity tearfully cried as she pointed at her mother. "I was about to go to college and we were going to make a life for ourselves ... and ... and you just helped to rip him out of my life!" Charity then angrily marched into the living room.

"Charity, I never meant for this to hurt you." Margaret followed behind Charity and grabbed her arm, but she snatched it away. "I didn't *make* Milton leave," Margaret defended herself.

"But you sure opened the door for him," Charity snappily responded before trying to desperately calm herself down. "I know what he did was wrong and I've forgiven him for that, but how could you do that to me?" Charity patted on her chest. "I'm your daughter."

"Charity, listen—"

"No!"

There was a stark break of silence.

Charity then snatched her pocketbook from the sofa and then started for the door. "I loved him, Mama." She took a quick breath before correcting herself, "I *still* love him. And the guys I dated afterwards, I only dated because I was trying to get over him," Charity sorrowfully admitted with downcast eyes. She sniffled, clutching the doorknob. "I may not be all that you've wanted, but thank God I'm not you!" She slammed the door as she left.

Those words pierced Margaret and her chest burned with pain. The sting from Charity's brutal honesty left her speechless, one of the few times in life. Tears streamed from her eyes as she slid down onto the ivory and antique gold blend, tufted sofa. Margaret slowly pulled the decorative lumbar pillow from behind her back and held it in her arms. She squeezed the cushion, unconsciously digging her manicured nails through the fine threading she once took so much pride in buying. Nothing in that house was more important to her at that moment than mending the strained relationship with her middle daughter.

Margaret grabbed a piece of tissue from a nearby hand-carved wooden box and dried the tears from her flushed cheeks. Just then the house phone rang. She hesitantly reached for the cordless that was on the edge of the coffee table and placed it to her ear.

"Hello," she sniffled.

"Is Mr. or Mrs. Gerald Maxwell in?" the strange, unfamiliar voice inquired.

"This is Mrs. Maxwell," Margaret quietly answered, having successfully stifled her tears. "How may I help you?"

"I'm sorry to inform you ma'am, but your daughter has been in an accident."

"My daughter?" Margaret sought clarity as she had three to be concerned about.

"Yes ma'am, Joy Maxwell. She's here at County Memorial."

"Oh my God! I'm on my way!" Margaret shouted and then tossed the phone aside. "Oh, my baby," she cried as she grabbed her coat and purse from the kitchen and rushed out the door.

Chapter Ten

"Where's my daughter? Where's Joy?" Margaret frantically asked an attendant seated behind the Emergency Room front desk.

"Ma'am, I need you calm down," a nurse who had just walked up instructed Margaret. Her eyes then shifted to Gerald's before landing back on Margaret. "What's your daughter's last name?"

"Maxwell. Her name is *Joy Maxwell*," Gerald spoke up. He had rushed right over from a neighborhood store when Margaret called him as she left home.

"Mama, Daddy?" a voice called from behind them.

"Oh thank God you're okay!" Margaret grabbed Joy by the arms and hugged her. She ecstatically swung her from side to side and the backpack on Joy's shoulder dropped to the floor.

"*Mama*," Joy's voice quivered from Margaret's jolting. "If you don't stop, I may need to stay here after all." She then giggled.

"Margaret, let the child breath," Gerald interjected with a smile as he pulled Joy away from her so that he could get a hug. After he released his embrace, he glared at her with questions in his eyes.

"What, Daddy?" Joy shyly looked at her father.

"Where is your phone?" he demanded to know. "You're obviously okay. There's a reason why you didn't call us."

"It got knocked out of my hands when I wrecked." Joy diminished the gravity of what had happened.

"What do you mean knocked out of your hands?" Margaret repeated, determined to get a straight answer out of her. "Were you sending text messages when the accident happened?"

"I'm sorry, nobody was hurt." She complacently shrugged.

Margaret had to bite her tongue in lieu of telling Joy off in public. She already had one strained relationship in the household; it took some strength to not add to that tally in one night.

"You talk to her Gerald because I can't." Margaret crossed her arms, trying to keep her composure.

"Joy, have you forgotten about what happened to your cousin? What were you thinking?" Gerald drove his point home.

Joy saw the hurt and seriousness in her mother's eyes also echoed in her father's. At that moment she reflected on the fact that it could have been a pedestrian, like her cousin who had died the previous year from someone texting and driving, and not a utility pole. It could have meant her life instead of her escape. The disappointment on her parents' faces put her blasé attitude in check.

"I'm sorry, Mama." Joy hugged her mother again while pulling her father closer. "I'll never do it again," she cried.

Gerald abstained from scolding her further, realizing that Joy had finally recognized her mistake. Knowing that she wasn't getting another car from them any time soon, Joy slowly handed over her keys.

The nurse having witnessed their exchange, nodded in approval. She had seen so many families come through the emergency room doors from senseless and avoidable accidents, not to mention how many injuries, even deaths that came as a result.

Gerald placed his hands on the counter and asked, "What do we owe you?"

The nurse gently smiled, looking on as Joy sobbed on her mother's shoulder. She then met eyes again with Gerald and responded, "I'm glad that you came down so quickly. Since she had her insurance card with her, we ran it and there isn't a charge at this time."

"Okay, thank you." Gerald signed the paperwork presented in front of him. "Will she need any medication? Is there a prescription?"

"Mr. Maxwell, your daughter came in a little shaken, so we evaluated her. She passed our screening assessments, but we did an additional examination to be sure," the nurse assured. "To tell you the truth, by the looks of the vehicle she was driving and the wreckage on the highway, your daughter is a walking miracle. The doctor has only prescribed medication for pain that she may need from soreness. Other than that, she's good."

"Thank God."

"Yes, God was with her," the nurse noted.

Before Gerald walked away he pondered the nurse's words. "You said by the looks of the vehicle, do you have pictures?" he inquired.

"Well, there was a news crew across the street covering an event when this happened," she replied, pointing to a flat screen TV in an upper corner of the waiting area wall. "See, it's already on the news."

There were photos of Joy's wrecked car splashed across the screen. The vehicle was practically wrapped around the pole. The reporter on the television informed that the jaws of life were used to pull the trapped teenager from inside.

"Joy, did you talk to anyone?" Margaret quietly asked.

"Just the lady who called 911 for me."

"Did she know who you were?" Margaret probed further.

"I think so because she asked me my name."

Margaret sighed and mumbled to herself, "Just what I *don't* need."

Gerald gazed at his wife before looking back to the nurse. "Thank you for everything."

"You're welcome. You all have a good night," the nurse said and then picked up a ringing phone.

Margaret repeated her sentiment by mouthing the words *thank you* to the nurse before the three of them started for the parking lot. Gerald walked ahead of his wife and daughter and handed his ticket to the hospital valet. He told Margaret that he would have a friend ride back with him later to get her car. Once the man left to retrieve their car, Joy excused herself to go back inside to use the restroom. Gerald brushed the top of her head with his hand as she walked away.

"Don't be long," he said to her.

"I won't," Joy answered, wiping her face with the back of her hand.

As Joy reentered the building, Margaret told Gerald, "Charity knows everything now."

Gerald appeared relieved. "Well, I'm glad it's all out in the open now."

"But she didn't take it too well."

Gerald nodded knowingly. "I'll talk to her when the time is right."

Margaret folded her arms across her chest as the wintry breeze picked up. "I think it's time for me to step down from being DA." It was as if it pained her to say it, but she knew it was the right time. She could no longer live this life for her mother who was now gone. It was time to live the dreams she had set for herself and to do it with a clear conscious, and also to be there for her family.

As she reflected on the argument she had with Charity and the accident Joy had just escaped, Margaret realized that in each instance she was concerned about her image. Over the years, she had slowly become someone she didn't want to be. It was time to go back to the days when things were simpler and more enjoyable. Not necessarily easy, but meaningful to her and to those closest to her.

Margaret sighed and looked into her husband's eyes, the one who had been her childhood sweetheart since they were twelve years old and thought true love was buying each other pineapple Now & Later, Lemonhead, and Boston Baked Beans candy. The one for whom she bore children. The one who promised to be there until death do them part.

"For better or for worse?" she asked, already knowing the answer.

And Gerald predictably answered, "For better or for worse."

Chapter Eleven

"It'll break her heart if you do that. Please, if you truly care about her, don't do it," Kim pleaded with her brother.

Milton paced the floor in his sister's apartment, having shared with her the possibility of ending things with Charity.

"I saw how she looked at you in church that Sunday. And she's always been nice to me, despite the way you treated her."

"But it seems as if our relationship may do more harm than good." Milton sighed. "Mama is mad at Mrs. Maxwell and Mrs. Maxwell, from what I know, said some things to her that she just can't get over. Daddy acts like he's caught somewhere in the middle while I'm trying to rekindle something with a woman who's at the center of it all."

Kim sighed as she stroked the back of her puppy that was propped in her arms. "Why did you even ask her for another chance then?"

"Because I'm a different person now."

"How Milton, if you're actually thinking about leaving her again?"

"I don't know." Milton rubbed the top of his head as he dropped down on the couch in front of the television set. "It seems as if everybody else thinks I'm that way. People do change."

Kim placed a hand on her brother's shoulder as she stood behind the sofa. "Do you hear yourself?"

He looked back at her with a bend in his face. "What?"

"I asked if you heard yourself." Kim returned his sour expression as she placed her puppy on the floor.

Milton turned back around and faced the television set that was showing a Thursday night game where Joshua Maxwell's team was playing.

"I asked you a question." Kim walked around the sofa and sat down beside him.

"What do you mean?"

Kim looked him squarely in the eyes and asked, "Do you remember when Daddy was running for office the first time?"

"Yeah, but what does that have to do with anything?"

"Don't you remember when some people tried to slander his name?"

Milton widened his eyes at Kim, motioning with his hands for relevance. "Okay, and?"

"Did he quit? Did he just throw in the towel because of what *other people* thought about him?" Kim raised an eyebrow. "Are you going to let other people make you lose the woman you say that you love?"

Milton intertwined his fingers and then tapped his thumbs together. He knew that Kim's question didn't require a vocal answer as his face told it all. He realized that if he allowed anything or anyone to come between him and Charity this time, there wouldn't be another.

Milton grunted as he pushed the OFF button on the remote. He reached for his duffel bag that he had been living out of for the past two days and started for the door.

"So, what are you going to do?" Kim curiously asked.

Milton stared at her and with a blank expression, honestly replied, "I don't know."

"Everything is beautiful. Mama really did her thing," Charity admitted, reflecting on the heart-to-heart conversation she had with Margaret since Joy's accident. "I think this may be her best display yet."

The decorations for the gala were beautifully draped around the building that was donated for the event by the owner. The adjoining dining room where they would feast burst with vibrant colors and a jubilant Christian theme.

"And did you see the tables with the beautiful centerpieces? Oh my goodness, I thought I had just walked into the cover of an elegant decorating magazine," she carried on. "And guess what else?"

Milton looked at her with a blasé expression painted across his face. "What's that?"

"The place cards have my designs on them!" Charity seemed excited beyond words. "I expected the programs to have them, but the place cards even have written on the back *designed by Charity Maxwell*," she sung in a jolly tone, and then proudly added, "along with my website. If I get to design for your friend retiring from the military, that's even more business for me!" She bounced in place, gently clapping her hands together.

Milton half-heartedly smiled as he slowly dragged his hand over his neatly cut goatee. "That's great," he somberly said.

Charity's enthusiasm dissolved with his dismal response. "Is everything okay?" she carefully asked.

"Can we talk?"

"Sure," Charity apprehensively replied. She followed him to the edge of the stage where they had just finished their final rehearsal run-through for the short play they were to perform in the cantata.

Milton helped Charity down to where he sat on the edge of the stage. He sighed as he took her hand.

"What is it?" Her eyes melted into a pool of concern.

"Well," Milton began, but then stole a moment for himself. "I was just wondering if things were settled between you and your mom." He didn't want to be the reason for causing a rift between them. "We didn't talk much about it yesterday since you spent the day with Joy."

"Well, we did have a candid talk about everything. Daddy really put things into perspective for me." She gently touched Milton's forearm. "He could always get me to see things more clearly."

"How so?" Milton wondered.

Charity pulled in a deep breath and exhaled. "In a nutshell, he pretty much asked me how I would have felt if Mama had been in an accident instead of Joy."

"Wouldn't it have been just as bad?" Milton's face spilled with confusion.

"Let me explain." She chuckled lightheartedly. "Basically, what he was saying is that Joy and I are on good terms, but I had just had an awful argument with Mama. I said some things that I'm sure hurt her probably worse than she had me. If she had been injured or God forbid killed, how would I have dealt with that?" Charity's eyes misted as she said, "I would have never gotten a chance to say that I'm sorry. And that's all she was trying to do … apologize for what she had done."

Milton cradled Charity in his arms. As she rested her head on his chest, he realized her commitment to him despite what her family thought. Although Charity had joked about making him wait until Christmas to reveal whether she'll be with him long-term or not, he was confident of her decision. They shared a bond that had withstood so much opposition, but remained unbreakable.

"Can we pray about our mothers?" Charity sincerely asked him. "This is Christmas time and I really want us all to celebrate *together*."

"Of course," Milton replied without hesitation. "Did you want to do the honor?"

Charity's dimples deepened as she smiled. "I guess I can since you did last time." She lowered her head and poured her heart out to God.

Milton immediately discarded the second thoughts he had about their relationship. When he came to his senses, he recognized that he could have lost Charity forever, not because of something he had done, but because of what other people thought about them.

Forever, he thought. The chance was too great to lose someone like her again … and that was not a risk he was willing to take.

Chapter Twelve

Francine watched television as Margaret formally announced stepping down as DA for the city of Lewiston Springs. Francine saw something different about the woman who had said those awful things about her family. Margaret's demeanor was humble even after several reporters hurled accusatory questions about Joy's texting and driving accident. Margaret was calm and faced their snide remarks with grace. She knew that Joy had made a mistake, and that was more of a reason why she needed to be there for her daughter. Her work caseload provided little time for her family, although she had managed to hold things together for so long.

"This city deserves a better DA, one who wants to be in this position one hundred percent," Margaret explained. "For so many years I've done what was expected of me from other people," she reflected on her mother, "but I need to do what's best for me." Margaret gently moved a few strands of hair from her eyes. "My mother was a philanthropist in this town and in her honor I would like to carry that torch."

Margaret was blessed in so many ways and she realized that her mother did the best she could and raised her in a way that she'd be able to support herself without having to work three jobs like she had. For that, Margaret was grateful. "So, in honor of Josie Henderson, my late mother, I would like to invite everyone again to the Christmas gala."

People began to whisper among themselves. It baffled them because that invitation had already been extended. Many patrons had already decided that they wouldn't be able to attend because of the ticket costs, regardless of the proceeds going to charity. Many wanted to rub elbows with the city elites, but making sure that their lights stayed on with food in the refrigerator was top priority.

Margaret saw the confused looks on some of their faces while others simply shook their heads. She then smiled as she announced, "Oh, did I forget to mention that it's free? For everybody!"

Immediate smiles invaded the faces of many while others laughed with joy. Even Laurence who had attended to support Margaret clapped as he stood alongside Gerald. Margaret's eyes met with Laurence who nodded and gave a thumbs up and she returned the gesture. Her eyes then shifted to Gerald who mouthed the words *I love you*. Margaret lovingly mouthed the words back.

Originally, the ticket sales were going to be donated to a local charity, but this year Margaret decided with Laurence's approval that the city was their charity. With so many who have never been to a classy affair, they wanted to do something really special, something that they'd remember for years to come.

With a farewell wave to the crowd, Margaret left them with these words, "Merry Christmas, everybody!"

"Charity, five minutes before you go on. We have a packed house, so give them what you gave me on last night." Marshall, the jubilant director winked.

Charity nervously smiled as she peeked at the crowd from behind the blue curtains. The children were singing *Joy to the World* with such high energy that as Charity listened her nervousness fizzled away. The confidence she'd had in rehearsal had returned and she was ready to deliver a performance even God would be proud of because she was doing it from the heart without any lingering animosity.

"Are you ready?" Milton came up behind Charity and placed his arms around her shoulders.

Her giddiness couldn't be hidden. She blushed with the coyness of a young school girl as she replied, "Yes, I am."

"You'll never guess who's here?"

Charity shrugged, staring Milton in the eyes, searching for some sort of clue. "Who?"

"My mother." Milton pulled the curtain back slightly just as Charity had done only moments ago and there on the front row next to Gerald and Margaret was Francine beside Laurence. The two, Margaret and Francine, looked as if they were apologizing with hand gestures that ended in a seated hug.

"Look at God work," Charity said, knowing that their prayer was heard.

"I know. I'm glad to see this is all finally behind us."

"What if they hadn't worked things out, would you have second thoughts about us?" Charity smiled as she peered into his eyes, oblivious to Milton's conversation with Kim.

"Maybe," Milton nonchalantly said with a grin.

"Excuse me?" Charity playfully hit him on the chest.

He laughed, trying to shield himself from the next hit she was about to deliver. "Maybe just second thoughts, but I wouldn't have the heart to act on it," he truthfully replied.

Charity nodded knowingly as she said, "That's what I needed to hear." She then looked away as a wardrobe person meticulously tugged at her clothing.

The woman took her turn at straightening Milton's outfit as well before hurrying away to a choir member whose robe needed pinning.

"Before we go out there, Charity, I just want to say thank you for giving me another chance."

"Who told you that I was giving you another chance?"

Milton cocked his head to one side. "Say what?" His mouth hung open.

"Christmas isn't for another few days." With a serious look, Charity pushed his chin up to close his mouth. "But I'll let you know before the night is over."

"You two are on," Marshall interrupted their conversation and ushered Milton and Charity out on stage.

As the final scene came to a close, Charity modestly bowed from the standing ovation, having played the part like a seasoned silver screen actress. Milton held her hand as they took another bow together. The two looked at their families gathered on the front row excitedly clapping their hands.

As the bright lights beamed onto their faces, Charity leaned in Milton's direction and whispered in his ear, "Okay, I guess you can be my boyfriend." She winked as he simply chuckled, shaking his head.

Just then light snow flurries began to descend delicately from the sky. Charity noticed it through the large windows as did Milton and many others in the crowd.

"*Snow in Mississippi?*" Charity murmured. Milton squeezed her hand and gently smiled. "I guess tonight is special in more ways than one."

Charity blushed as she returned his loving gaze.

It was decided, he was not only her Christmas beau, but her love always. Charity continued gazing at Milton and inwardly thanked God for their reunion. Just weeks ago, she would have never imagined that this was what her Christmas vacation held. Milton had redeemed himself, and now she couldn't see herself with anyone else. Tonight was a success in many respects, but in her world particularly with Milton.

Charity was indeed his leading lady, now and forever.

Love suffers long and is kind; love does not envy; love does not parade itself, is not puffed up; does not behave rudely, does not seek its own, is not provoked, thinks no evil; does not rejoice in iniquity, but rejoices in the truth; bears all things, believes all things, hopes all things, endures all things.

1 Corinthians 13:4-7

A Note from the Author

Merry Christmas everyone...

Over the years, I've seen (have even used it in the past not realizing what I was doing) the words Merry Xmas. In recent years, it didn't seem like a simple abbreviation, but a deletion of my Savior. Interestingly, take note of Who the "X" replaces ... "Christ." We cannot take Christ out of the equation, if and when many do, this changes the entire meaning—well, it makes it meaningless. Some stores peddle off holiday cards that show a merry Santa Claus giving gifts to little children, dismissing the greatest gift God gave to us. What does Christmas mean to the average American?

Many argue that it has paganistic roots while others take advantage of this day to siphon money from unsuspecting Christians. It's obviously clear that the motive behind celebrating this day may vary depending upon who you ask. For me and my family, Christmas is not centered on gift-giving; it is centered on Christ. We give of our time, our efforts, and our love. We often laugh, recalling that it's not our birthday that we're celebrating, but Christ's. We do share a token of appreciation with one another whether it is a card, a phone call, or something that we may need or can afford to give, but that is also practiced all year round, not just because the country has deemed December 25th a national holiday.

Also, it's important to not go into debt trying to impress someone with a present that you can't even afford. How is that a gift? It may leave you feeling empty and the other person guilty because of the amount of money spent. Consider the hungry, the homeless, and the imprisoned.

"Then the King will say to those on His right hand, 'Come, you blessed of My Father, inherit the kingdom prepared for you from the foundation of the world: for I was hungry and you gave Me food; I was thirsty and you gave Me drink; I was a stranger and you took Me in; I was naked and you clothed Me; I was sick and you visited Me; I was in prison and you came to Me.' "Then the righteous will answer Him, saying, 'Lord, when did we see You hungry and feed You, or thirsty and give You drink? When did we see You a stranger and take You in, or naked and clothe You? Or when did we see You sick, or in prison, and come to You?' And the King will answer and say to them, 'Assuredly, I say to you, inasmuch as you did it to one of the least of these My brethren, you did it to Me,'" Matthew 25:34-40, NKJV.

In the bustle of storewide sales and preparing dinners fit for kings, let us not forget about the King of kings and Lord of lords, Jesus Christ. He didn't forget about us.

Please enjoy an excerpt from the next installment of The True Love Novellas: *Single, Saved, & Searching.*

❤ ❤ ❤

He who finds a wife finds a good thing,
and obtains favor from the Lord.
~Proverbs 18:22

Chapter One

Strong, black, educated, and responsible—those are the characteristics Elisha would love to have in man, to name a few. Blinded to the world's standard of beauty, he'd be resourceful enough to create his own. Stand as a model of independence, an example of strength, an advocate of loyalty, and a pillar of integrity.

As she stared at her boyfriend through squinted eyes, Elisha wondered if she was asking for too much. Her friend Gina had told her yes while her other friend, Tonia, had emphatically declared no. Caught up somewhere in the middle Elisha wondered, *what does my man say*? After a dismissive grunt, she knew that he'd say he possessed all of those qualities and then some. But in her eyes, that was far from the truth.

Chauncey McDaniel was strong in the sense that he bench pressed more than her and one of her girlfriend's weight, but when it came to knowing God's Word and standing up for Biblical principles, he fell short. He certainly was black, as dark as they came, but not as educated as she would like and certainly not responsible enough to introduce him to her parents. Chauncey's family was rich and he pretty much had everything handed to him, but the wealth still didn't comfort Elisha enough to completely abandon her values.

"Why are you so quiet?" Elisha asked, noticing that Chauncey hadn't spoken three words to her since they got inside of one of his prized possessions, a red convertible Porsche 911 Carrera Cabriolet. "Did you have too much to drink?"

"If I had too much to drink, would you be on the passenger side? Don't say stupid things that don't make sense." He callously shook his head.

"I don't even know why I'm with you. All of sudden you're a drunk. You never drank when we first started dating." Elisha sucked her teeth. "Leave it up to you to ruin a perfectly good evening." She cut her eyes away from him and with folded arms sunk down into the soft leather-trimmed heated seating.

Chauncey grunted under his breath and then tightened his lips again. Soon, he took the last busy street before the secluded, residential road Elisha lived on. After he parked in front of her garage, the neighbors who lived next door were just pulling out of their driveway. Chauncey casually waved as did Elisha before the neighbors disappeared out of sight. Chauncey then carefully looked at the darkened house across the street that shared the wooded dead end as Elisha's home.

"Are they out of town again?" he questioned, as they stood at the front of his car.

Elisha glanced back and then remembered, "Oh yeah, I told them that I'd turn the lights on for them tonight." She reached inside of her handbag and began fidgeting with the keys on her ring, and then started down her driveway.

Chauncey grabbed her by the arm and yanked her back. "That can wait." The force in his voice was tighter than the grip on her arm. "I told you that we'd talk at home."

With slightly parted lips, Elisha's gaze on him drifted down to the hand he held her with.

"Now get inside." His voice demonized as he commanded, snatching her towards the front steps. Chauncey looked back one last time before he slammed the door behind them.

To enjoy more of *Single, Saved, & Searching* order your copy today wherever books are sold.

About the Author

RENEE MCCOY (known to readers as Renée Allen McCoy) is a loving wife and mother, an author, but most importantly a devoted Christian. Having traveled to many parts of the world, today she, her husband, and their two children make Mississippi home. She maintains a newsletter, *Straight Up*, and a devotional blog, *In His Name*.

To date, she has penned seven books that include: The Fiery Furnace series (*The Kiss of Judas*, *Confessions*, and *The Eleventh Hour*), *Soul Ties: Breaking Up with a Past That's Killing Your Future* (non-fiction), *The Christmas Beau* (The True Love Novellas, Book 1), *In the Presence of My Enemies*, and *Single, Saved, & Searching* (The True Love Novellas, Book 2). Renée has also written for the world renowned pocket devotional, *The Upper Room*, both in digital and print.

With a heart to tell stories that will not only entertain, Renée hopes to enlighten readers to capture the message and power of God's saving grace.

Visit her online at www.ReneeAllenMcCoy.com for more information on the third book in The True Love Novellas series, *A Test of Faith*.

FaytheWorks is an independent Christian publishing company that produces fiction and non-fiction titles. Since its formation, the goal has been and will always remain to share Christ focused stories and testimonies with the world. With a solid foundation on the Holy Bible, the infallible Word of God, we believe that Jesus Christ is Lord.